TURTLE
HEAVEN

TURTLE HEAVEN

Joshua Culley

NP
NEWPROTEST
PUBLISHING

This book is primarily dedicated to my father, without whom there would be no story.

It's also dedicated to my wife, Kendra, who put up with me while I wrestled with this text for years. Thank you for your patience.

Lastly, this book is dedicated to everyone who bears the impossible weight of not being enough.

We are the narrators of the stories of our lives. We are free to annotate our tragic pasts with lessons we've learned. We can include new learnings in the footnotes.

We can even write a whole new book.

Author's Note

This novel is fiction. But it is mostly true.

Turtles to Save

Summer, 1984.

Just before noon, Josh's seatbelt squeezed across his lap, and his arms and legs jerked forward. Crayons and a screwdriver tumbled off the seat next to him, clattering onto the dirty floorboard of the old pickup truck. The stench of burning rubber filled the cab as the truck skidded to a halt, kicking a cloud of dust into the hot New Mexico air. Uncle Randy flung open the driver's door and sprinted across the highway.

Josh smudged his little face against the truck window. He scrunched his nose and giggled as his wiry uncle dashed, bowlegged, towards the center of the road. Uncle Randy looked just like Dad, mimicking his same silly motions, the half-cigarette bobbing between his lips.

Uncle Randy glanced up and down the long stretch of dusty highway. He reached down and snatched something off the asphalt before hurrying back to the truck.

"What is that, Uncle Randy?" Josh craned his little neck to see over the bench seat, but it was hard to see much of anything.

"Hey Sam, check it out. Just like the old days, huh?" Uncle Randy called out. He passed the object to his passenger and revved the engine.

Sam laughed from the passenger seat and turned the object over in his hands several times. "Yeah! That's a pretty good-sized one!"

"What is it, Daddy?" Josh leaned forward, tapping the seat in front of him. "I can't see it!"

Sam turned to Josh with a soft smile. "Check it out, Joshua!" He handed the object to the boy. The truck lurched forward and veered back onto the highway, causing Josh to nearly lose his grip. He tightened his hold and settled back in his seat.

The object was mostly round, bumpy, and mottled with streaks of brown and yellow. Josh's eyes grew wide. He had never seen a real turtle shell before. He traced his little fingers across the geometric patterns on the ridges of the shell's crown and then flipped it over to see the smooth, yellow underside. He nearly jumped in his seat when he saw the claws and tail tucked tightly against the turtle's body.

"Daddy, look! It's a real turtle shell!" He held the shell high and flipped it over several times to show every angle.

"Careful, Joshua. Don't drop it." Sam reached back and touched Josh's shoe. "It's delicate."

Josh pulled the shell back to his lap and nodded. "I'll be real careful, Daddy. Hey Uncle Randy, is the turtle alive?"

"Oh, probably," Randy called back, laughing. He took a swig from a half-empty can of Coca-Cola. "Just hold onto it and wait a second, Joshy. Just watch it."

The little boy gasped when the turtle extended its neck from its shell. The turtle looked at Josh and then pushed its feet against the boy's hand. He giggled when the turtle's tiny claws pricked his palm and tickled him. Josh gently touched the turtle's head and laughed when it ducked back into its shell.

"It's so funny, Daddy!" He held the turtle up again but then drew it back to his lap when he remembered to be careful.

"It's a box turtle, Joshua. It can completely hide inside the shell to protect itself."

"Even from cars?"

"No, not from cars. That's why your Uncle Randy picked it up off the road. To keep it safe." He touched Josh's foot again and squeezed it.

"Box turtle," Josh mouthed the words back to his dad. He wiggled his foot free from his dad's hand and brushed the shell with his tiny fingertips. "B-O-X turtle," he spelled to himself. He looked up and watched the world zip past the smudged window, and he wondered if there were any other turtles to save on the highway.

Seven

Summer, 2016.

I'm daydreaming again. I was just in my office, but I think the white noise from the air conditioner has lulled me out of my desk chair. The red accent wall in my office dissolves into thin silk threads, like a spider's web, and I can see the forest of dense evergreen trees behind it. Now the office is gone, and I can feel moist air blowing across my face. I'm floating through the air, drifting between cedars and Douglas fir trees, and then I gently, so gently, touch the ground with my bare feet.

Now I'm standing on bright, almost-glowing moss, and it's cool and soft between my toes. Water drips from my hair. It's running down my forehead. The droplets fall and splash the top of mushroom caps on the forest floor. I close my eyes and hear familiar bird songs cut through the hissing rain.

The woods move with life. Fiddlehead ferns unfurl and spin open endlessly, like emerald fractals pouring their gleaming eternity onto the forest floor. The air shimmers with glints of light. Every drop of rain catches blades of sunlight that pierce the canopy.

Am I moving through the forest, or is it moving around me? Am I the forest? How long have I been here?

There's a voice here in the background of the woods. I think it's been here with me the entire time. It feels like I'm eavesdropping on a conversation or perhaps some kind of presentation or speech. Something about finances. Responsibility. I try to ignore the voice and travel further through the trees, but the words grow clearer and difficult to ignore.

I should listen to it.

I focus and filter through the sounds of life in the woods. I quiet the hissing rain and then silence the birds. There's a river, too, and I force it to grow quiet until it barely ripples. I listen more closely to the voice. When I do, the trees around me vanish into colorful smoke. The birds are gone, but there are feathers everywhere. The moss dries out and turns into brown commercial carpet, and I feel myself falling out of my daydream and back into the office. The sunlight that streamed through the forest canopy grows garish and becomes the fluorescent tube lights above my head.

I recognize this voice. It's *mine*. I'm the one giving the presentation.

"This is an important decision you're making. Not just for

you and your child, but perhaps—" I pause and press my lips together. I lean forward. I gently nod in my best attempt to appear sage. "But perhaps for your future grandkids as well. This kind of thing changes a family for generations. It creates generational wealth."

I've given this same speech three times this week. It's only Tuesday. I run my hand over a large bronze turtle on my desk and pat the shell. *"Slow and steady* deposits into your retirement account so you can achieve your dreams." I nod towards the wife and then back at the husband. "And the life insurance in place to make sure your family succeeds, even if — God forbid — something happens to you."

I wait a few seconds and brush the wet cedar branches from my mind. I know what's going to happen next. He's going to reach over and gently touch her hand. Their eyes will meet, and then they'll both look at me and nod. Yup, there it is. I smile back at them and slowly nod in agreement. It would be heartwarming if this exact scene hadn't played out a hundred times in my office already.

"I'll have Pattie draft up the documents to sign. You're on your way to financial security." The same closing lines. The same e-mail fired off to the office manager. The same documents to print and sign. Two or three appointments every day, Monday through Thursday. Week in, week out. Packaged. Condensed. Memorized.

I steal a glance at the clock above my clients' heads while

they talk to each other. This meeting took twenty minutes. Twenty minutes, and half the time was spent floating through the Olympic National Forest. Pattie brings in the documents to sign and sets the packet in front of them, and I thank her. I point to the signature lines and say the next set of words in my script. It's like speaking an incantation. With the words of the spell in the air, I start slipping back into the woods.

I force a blink and shake my head to keep my mind in the office, and then I run my thumbnail against the raised characters on my pen to feel the imprinted letters: *Joshua Brennan, Insurance Agency Owner.*

That's who I am, right? This is who I'm supposed to be. I dig my thumbnail deeper and watch the clients sign their documents.

I've been an insurance agency owner for about five years in this little Central Valley California town. This is my first business. Before this, I never sold a thing in my life. I never had employees of my own. I had no idea what I was doing when I started.

And now? After clawing my way up the steep learning curve, I've figured out the marketing and sales, and I have simple and repeatable office processes.

Repeatable.

Repeatable.

Maybe that's the problem.

"Pattie just e-mailed you a calendar invite for your policy

review for next year. We'll see how the retirement account is behaving and decide together if we need to make any adjustments. Maybe we'll increase contributions and bump up that life insurance if you decide to have another baby!" I smile at the wife, and she laughs. I knew she would. I already asked them if they planned to have more kids when I went through the sales pitch, and she said she wanted to. The husband said he wasn't sure. They will. And they'll increase the life insurance coverage next year.

I wave goodbye to the young couple as they leave the air conditioned office and head back outside into the California heat. They're in their early twenties, just starting their lives. Everything is a new adventure for them. They're still in that state of wonder at how the financial world works. I'm 37. My wife and I have been married 14 years, and when it comes to insurance and financial services, I've got it figured out. I want to help my customers figure it out as well.

Everything in my life is appropriately set up, organized, and safe. Steady. *Slow and steady.*

But something feels off. Maybe I'm supposed to be doing something else. I close my eyes and trace the smooth ridges on the bronze turtle shell. I let myself drift back into the woods.

"You're home early, hon," Kendra calls from the kitchen. She's facing the oven, and the whole house smells like freshly baked bread. Her long brown hair is twisted into the neck straps of her flour-dusted apron.

"Yeah, I don't think I'm gonna get more work done at the office today." I approach her and gently untangle her hair from the strap. She kneads the ball of dough like she's creating life with her hands, shaping and folding it and smashing it back into the countertop.

"Oh? How come? Did your appointment not go well?" She spins around and kisses me. "Or did you just want to... spend some extra time with me?" She raises her eyebrows up and down, teasing me.

"Ha! Baby, it's barely noon. The kids are running around the house!"

"So?" She presses even closer, and I breathe in her perfume and bread flour.

I lean in and kiss her, and I feel her whole body relax. She places her hand on my chest, and then she nudges me away.

"Thanks! That's all I needed. I still have more bread to make." She grins, and when she spins back around, the flour flies up and sparkles around her like fairy dust.

"Oh, so you *are* teasing me?" I keep my hand on her waist and try to pull her back to me, but she wriggles free and returns to her dough. "Fine, fine," I protest. "Anyhow, the appointment went well. I landed it. Two terms and an IRA. Pretty simple deal."

"Well, good job, honey. You always do well." She opens the oven, pulls out a pan of golden brown rolls, and then sets them on the counter. "This batch needs to sit, but you can help me load stuff into the RV."

I can barely think past the smell of hot rolls. I draw a deep breath and close my eyes.

"Something wrong?" Kendra peers over her shoulder while she splits the next batch of dough into little balls.

"No, I'm just taking it in. The bread smells so good. It smells like home."

I haven't told her about my daydreams or longing for the trees and the rain. I haven't told her how much I miss *that* home. It's been nearly seven years.

"Alright, Kendra. Which basket needs to go?"

"Both, but take the one with the condiments first. I still have a lot to load into the other one."

I drag the basket closer to me and rummage through it. Ketchup, mustard, mayo, deli-meats. A tub of sprouts. A stack of paper plates. "Oh, sandwich fixings."

"Yeah, most of this bread is for sandwiches. I think that basket is done, though."

"Are you going to put the rest of the kitchen into the other basket? How long is this road trip supposed to last?"

Kendra has been planning our "Great American Road Trip" for months, plotting out all the places she visited as a child. We'll see the Grand Canyon, Mt. Rushmore, Old Faithful at Yellowstone, and a few other places along the way. I've lost track of all the destinations she's mentioned.

"I'm not really sure. A few weeks? But it'll be longer than the amount of food we're bringing. We'll have to stop by a few grocery stores."

We'll pile into the old RV in a few days and hit the road. Maybe this adventure is what I need. Something new. Something different.

"Alright. I'll take this to the RV and grab some tools from the shop. I need to crawl under the engine and make sure everything looks alright."

"Ok, Mr. Insurance man. But kiss me first!"

I kiss her again, and then stop to brush the flour off my shirt.

"Holy smokes, Mrs. *Baker* woman. Now I need to go find Mrs. *Laundry* woman to clean this mess off my clothes!" She gasps and then swings a fist at my shoulder. I dodge out of the way and grab the basket.

"Listen here, Mr. Jerk-face! You can load a washing machine yourself. You can even put your dirty clothes *into* the hamper instead of next to the bed!" She scrunches up her face, and I see a cute streak of flour dusting her forehead.

"Alright, alright!" I dodge another punch and rush to the front door with the basket.

Outside, the heat has climbed another few degrees. The asphalt up the street is covered in mirage, and I imagine desert wanderers chasing illusory pools of water in vain. I feel my sweat evaporating off my skin, and I raise and lower my eyebrows to feel the crackle of crystallizing salt on my forehead. The short walk from the front door to the driveway is the distance between desert sand dunes.

I want to turn around and head back into the air-conditioned house. This California heat is intolerable. It's cruel to have to live here. Seven years, and I still haven't gotten used to it.

After walking the desert driveway, I open the RV door. The vehicle is a beast, stretching 30 feet long and nearly eight feet wide. It takes up the whole length of my driveway. I don't know how tall it is, but it has to be at least twice my height. I'm supposed to maneuver this behemoth across the country with less than two feet of clearance on either side of the lane as we roar down the freeway. The front wheels look too narrow and small to hold the RV's weight. They're almost comically small.

I step up into the RV, and a mass of hotter air envelops me. My throat, nose, and eyes immediately shut to protect my organs from broiling, and I wonder if I'm going to pass out. I swallow a tiny breath and think about the tragic weekly news stories of parents who left their children in their cars in this heat. Pets, too. I set the basket down on the pop-out table and crank open the air vents on the ceiling. I don't think we humans or animals are designed for these temperatures.

There are three vents to open in the ceiling. It's an oven through the whole length of the vehicle. I walk past the faded teal-blue upholstery and purple and pink streaks on the walls, and it brings me back to the strangely-colored days of the 1990s. High school was awash in contrasting colors, sharp angles, and high-top shoes. Good days. It wasn't hot back then. Not in Washington, anyway.

Kendra plans to paint over the 1990s walls in the RV. Probably gray, like the house. She enjoyed renovating the kitchen and laundry room with me, and she discovered a gray paint that goes with everything. It's even called *Agreeable* Gray. I wonder how it will look against the faded teal.

I tug on the ceiling vent in the rear bedroom. It's stuck. I think the plastic is heat-baked. If I keep pulling on it, it's probably going to break. After a few minutes of struggling, it finally budges and cranks, but I'm sweating from concentrating so hard. The tiny bit of air that moves through the vent doesn't help, and I'm exhausted from my heat-soaked exertion. I drag myself back to the front of the vehicle and run my hands along the purple streaks on the wall.

I used to disagree with Kendra about paint colors, but she's never been wrong. Not even once. Early in our marriage, I told her I wanted orange walls in our house. I argued that I should have the final say because I made more money. After fighting about it, she gently convinced me that I was being stubborn for no reason, and that I didn't care about the wall colors. She's the one who had the opinion, and I was just being contrary. She was right. So naturally, the RV is going to have Agreeable Gray walls. It will be like an extension of our house, so we'll always feel like we're home, no matter where we are. That's probably better than being stuck in the 1990s on our road trip, although the music would be amazing.

I open the fridge door to load the condiments. As I grab the BBQ sauce and Dijon mustard, I wonder how many different kinds of sandwiches she plans to make. For Kendra, "roughing it" always involves a fully stocked fridge, her own silverware and dishes, a very high thread-count sheet-and-pillowcase set, and an assortment of hair appliances. It's nothing like the tenting I did as a kid. "Roughing it" means something different to everybody, I suppose.

The chilled air from the fridge pours over my hand and between my knuckles. It's like a frozen fog rolling over hills. I imagine standing on a field where I watch a mass of cold air collide with the intolerable heat, creating a tornado in the RV. Is it a tornado? Or is it a hurricane that forms when hot and cold air mix? I don't remember how it works, but the RV interior erupts into a lightning and hail storm. Searing winds threaten to rip the teal upholstery off the fold-out couch and draw it into the swirling, raging vortex.

A few weeks ago, Pattie interrupted one of my stories at the office. I'd often close out the afternoon with my thoughts about the current news or a story from my childhood. In this case, I was telling my staff about the third grade. I lived in an apartment in Steilacoom, and I was playing catch with my friends on the lawn between the buildings. Later in the afternoon, I discovered that my knees were green. I didn't know about grass stains yet, so I spent the remainder of the evening wondering if I was turning into a Teenage Mutant Ninja Turtle. I thought about having pizza delivered to my new sewer home and hanging out with other Ninja Turtles. I was excited but sad that I couldn't hang out with my school friends during the day anymore. That's the price of being a mutant crime fighter. These thoughts continued until I took a bath that evening. I was quite disappointed when I scrubbed the imaginary turtle scales off my knees.

Pattie interrupted my story to ask me if I spent a lot of time alone as a child. She's a great office manager. She knows what needs to be done in the office and gives me thoughtful feedback about the ideas I present to the team. I'm glad she was comfortable asking me this pointed question because it's the kind of question that most people *avoid* asking their bosses. It roughly translates to, "Your imagination was wild, and I'm not convinced you had any adults around to tell you this."

The tornado, or hurricane, finally fades in the RV, and the winds are slow enough for me to finish loading the fridge. I hold the door open for a few seconds to breathe the cold air. I nod. I *did* spend a lot of time alone as a child. I was a latchkey kid, so I had the freedom to let my imagination explore the universe. I battled terrible beasts during the day while my parents worked their day jobs, and I hid in terror from darker versions of those beasts at night while my parents worked their night jobs.

My friends wondered if I had parents at all. There were days when I wondered the same.

I open a few overhead cabinets on the way out of the RV to ensure they breathe, but I don't know if that's helpful. Maybe it's just letting more hot air in. Or is it letting the stuffy hot air out? I'm not sure.

We'll be packing for a while before we're ready to go, loading a couple week's worth of clothes and extra blankets. There's room for the medical kits and my survival go-bags, too. I'm sure Kendra will figure out how to fill every space in this rig.

I walk through the narrow aisle to the front of the vehicle and run my hand over the velour captain's chair. This is my seat. I'll sit here for hours, traveling from landmark to landmark, cruising on a highway that will look a little too narrow for the vehicle. I'll drive away from the office routine and this blasted heat. The kids will lounge on the couch, or play cards at the table, or sleep in the rear bedroom while I drive across the country. Kendra will make meals far too fancy for vacation, and we'll love it.

Outside, I look under the vehicle to check for oil leaks. It's dry under the engine and transmission. Even the oil pan is dry and dusty, which is rare for an old RV. I assumed I'd have to top off the oil every few hundred miles to keep up with leaks, but this vehicle is sealed. The undercarriage is roomy enough for me to peek under without laying on my back, and it all looks good.

This RV was such a bargain. The engine runs smoothly, no oil leaks, and the interior smells nice. There aren't any water stains from leaks on the roof, either. For a used motorhome we found on Craigslist, it's in excellent condition. It's a lot better than the 1970s RV we bought when we lived in Washington. That one leaked, and it smelled like it did, too.

After giving the RV another quick once-over, I return to the house to escape the heat. I'll grab my tools from the garage when it cools down tonight.

Once I'm back inside, I set the empty basket on the countertop and see Kendra loading the other basket with plastic cups and more plates.

"Hey Kendra, this RV is great. No leaks! I even—"

My phone interrupts me in Morse code: *dash, dot dot dash.*

"Which one was that?" She grabs more dishes for the basket.

"That's an *X*."

I've set my phone notifications to different Morse code letters. I like the conversation it generates when I'm in public. I've already used the "T" for Twitter and "E" for e-mail. I have to use "X" for text.

"Ok, but what does it say?"

I start to read the text, but the words are difficult to see. Is it my eyes? I force myself to blink through an eruption of cold, dense fog that fills the room, pouring out of the screen. My chest tightens, and I find myself slowly exhaling, unable to take any breath back into my lungs. My heart is a drum, pounding to a song I've never heard. I look up and meet Kendra's eyes.

"Well? Who texted you?"

The fog clears, but the pounding doesn't go away. I can still barely breathe.

"It's... my sister. Our dad is dying."

"What?!"

"That's what it says. Angie texted that I need to call our dad. He's dying."

I don't look up from the phone. I study the words on the screen to find some additional meaning in them. My dad is dying. I'm supposed to call him, but I don't know if he can answer. Is he injured? Is he sick? How does my sister know? She doesn't live close to him, so why would she know before I do?

"Are you going to call him?" Kendra rushes to my side. "Are you ok?" She touches my arm, but I pull away from her.

"I need to call my sister."

Kendra nods and steps back to let me pass. I drag my feet through the kitchen and the hallway and into our room so I can sit on the bed. I need to breathe. I can't breathe.

I stare at the call button on the screen. I don't remember the last time we spoke. It's been years. My thumb hovers over the call button to press it, but my hand refuses to obey. Nothing is working. I'm light-headed, and my vision is narrowing.

I don't know how much time passes before I finally make

the call. When I do, my sister immediately answers. "Hello?"

"Hey Angie, it's Josh." My voice is flat. Dispassionate. I don't sound like someone who just learned his father is dying. "What happened?"

"I know, it's awful. He called me." Her voice is strained. She's still crying.

I wait for her to find her words between sobs. Our dad is well enough to call her, so he's not incapacitated. This wasn't the result of an injury, probably. So he must be sick. Maybe cancer? I can see him in a hospital bed with tubes connected to his arms and face while he talks to my sister on the phone.

"He... he said not to tell you, Josh."

"Not tell me what?"

"He said not to tell you that he's dying."

There is a chasm between me and my half-sister. This chasm is a pit filled with uncertainty, confused expectations, fear, hope, and perhaps jealousy. My dad was *her* father first. She gets to claim that birthright, whatever good that is. But now? After divorces, remarriages and abandonment, our father belongs to neither of us. She and I are both the estranged children of a man neither of us know anymore.

Even so, I'm the most recent child. By every measure, he was my father longer. More recently. So why would our father choose to tell Angie that he was dying instead of me? When was the last time they talked?

I don't know if I'm angry. Maybe I'm hurt. Am I allowed to

feel that? I barely know my sister, but bitterness is growing in my throat right now, and I want to hang up. I'm supposed to feel grief over my dad, but hearing that he asked her not to tell me feels like a betrayal. But a betrayal of what? What was I expecting?

It's fine. I don't care.

I swallow down the bitterness and try to think of something else. I try to remember that I'm not the only one who is losing a father. She's allowed to have a relationship with him, whatever it is. I don't have to know about it. I don't have to understand why.

But why would he want to keep it from me? Was he planning to just die and have me find out later through an online link to an obituary? Through a grief-filled Facebook post from my sister? It's unfair. I grip my phone tighter to keep from throwing it across the room.

"Josh," Angie says, breaking the long silence. "He wanted to tell you. He's just afraid to let you know."

My grip on my phone relaxes, and the bitterness is diluted by warm grief. I'm still his son.

"Did Dad say how long he has left?" I ask, trying to hide my sense of relief.

"I'm going to take time off work to fly up there. But you definitely need to go soon. Are you able to go? He said he thinks he's going to die within the week."

My breath freezes in my chest, and I can't breathe again.

One week?

I tell my sister goodbye and hang up the phone. My heart is pounding, and my hands are sweating. I swallow, and my neck muscles struggle to relax. I don't remember the last time I felt this way. Shortness of breath. Rapid heartbeat.

I've been holding the air in my chest until my lungs burn. I force myself to exhale, and my breath is shaky as I blow it out through clenched teeth. I pull up my dad's phone number and stare at the dial button on the screen. With my eyes closed, I force myself to press the call button.

The phone rings.

How much more time does my dad have? Days? Hours? What happened? How can he be dying within a week?

The phone rings again.

When was the last real conversation I had with my dad? I've reached out a few times over the years, but it's been formal. Distant. The last time, we visited my dad in Portland. Kendra and I brought the girls to see him during one of our road trips from Olympia to Dinuba to visit Kendra's family. We stopped by to take my dad out to dinner and say hello. It was awkward.

The phone rings again.

Aside from the posts I've shared on Facebook, my father doesn't know much about me. He knows from pictures that I'm married and have three daughters. He knows that I'm an insurance agent. I've filled my Facebook profile with my car projects, political rants, and theological musings, but it's only a caricature. It's not really me. Not all of me. You can't have a relationship with a caricature.

I know even less about my dad. I was sixteen when he left; that was the last time he was my father-figure. What does a sixteen-year old know about their own father?

My dad finally answers. "Hi, Joshua!" He has more cheer in his voice than I expect. What was I expecting? I don't know how people are supposed to sound when they are dying.

"Hey, Dad. Angie told me."

There's a long pause. The silence lasts for so long that I pull the phone from my face to check if he's still on the line. He is, but he's not saying anything. Is he upset that I know and that I called him? Did he think Angie wouldn't tell me?

"Yeah," he says slowly, breaking the silence. "She didn't take it very well," he says, weaker this time. Much weaker. I can hear him wheeze, and it takes him a while to get through his words.

"She was still crying when I called her," I tell him.

Now it's my turn to draw out the silence. I don't want to say anything. I don't want him to say anything either, but I need to ask him about his condition. I need to know what he told Angie, but I know that when he brings the answer into existence, into this space between us, it will become real. The specter of Death will grow and fill every shadow. It will whisper from the echo of every unidentified sound at night. Death will start the hunt. It will pursue my father until he can't run anymore. And it will devour him.

I don't want to ask, but I don't have a choice. I can only hold the world in silence for so long. "So, Dad. What's... what's going on?"

"I'm going to die, son." His words are emotionless. But the words give birth to the darkness.

My father is going to die.

Sometimes, we see Death as a single figure, cloaked and skeletal. The Reaper. But sometimes, this time, Death is an unholy host of phantoms. They hang in the air, in every shadowed corner of my peripheral vision, and behind me. I try to block the words from my mind, but the phantoms chant it over and over: *Your father is going to die!*

They yell it at me: *Your father is going to die!*

They shriek and scream the curse into the air: *Your father is going to die!*

"How, Dad?"

"Well, my body is failing. Things are shutting down. I think this might be my last week."

I want to understand, but I don't want him to tell me anything more. I don't want to feed the phantoms with more words. I force the image of my frail and dying father out of my mind.

"We're going to drive up tonight so we can be there, hopefully by tomorrow afternoon."

"Oh, that's good. That should be enough time."

I have no idea if it's enough time or not. Some people with terminal cancer survive for months, even years. Some people don't make it more than a few days. I doubt my dad knows if it's enough time. Not even the phantoms know.

"I hope so. I'm bringing Kendra and the kids, too."

"Oh, that's great!" He coughs several times before continuing. "It will be good to see them, too."

When he says those words, I remember that I have to drag my wife and my daughters into this grief as well. Can I hide them from the darkness?

"Alright, Dad. I've got to get going. We've got a lot to pack."

"Ok, son. I'll see you tomorrow, then?" he asks, and his voice carries a hopeful lilt.

"Yeah. Tomorrow."

I hang up and set my phone on the bed next to me. I close my eyes.

Inhale.

Hold. One. Two. Three. Four. Five.

Exhale.

The tears don't come. I blink a few times to make sure, but my eyes are dry and unsympathetic. My heart is still racing. I breathe deeply again and brace myself for the flood of emotion, but I don't feel anything. I shake my head and walk back to the kitchen.

Kendra is waiting for me. Her eyes are swollen. As soon as she sees me, she wipes her eyes and throws her arms around me. "Are you ok, Josh?"

"Yeah, I'm fine." My shoulders stiffen under her embrace. "We have to change our road trip plans."

"I figured. We'll drive up to Oregon."

"We have to go right away. My dad said he's dying within the week."

"What?! A week? Ok." She furls her eyebrows and looks around the room. She sighs and then nods. "I mean, we'll have to pack a little faster then. We have a lot of work to do."

"Can we go tonight?" I press her. "I don't know how much time we have. I think we should."

"Josh, I don't think that's a good idea. We have so much to load."

"Are you sure? This is really important."

"There's no way. By the time we finish loading, it'll be late. We'll be exhausted. You'll be too tired to drive. We'll pack tonight and leave in the morning, ok?"

I know she's right. I'm drained as it is.

"Ok. Can you tell the girls? I don't think I'm ready to talk to them about it yet."

"We can just tell them that we're leaving tomorrow, and then we can tell them about your dad in the RV, ok? I don't think we have to stop and talk through it all with them right now." Kendra scoots another filled basket towards me. "Ok?"

Olivia, my oldest daughter, peeks from around the entrance of the kitchen. She's thirteen and old enough to understand death and grief. I can see the gears of youthful curiosity spinning in her head. Her mind is giving birth to questions.

"Talk to us about what?" she asks. Her eyebrows are raised. Delaying the story will take more effort than simply telling her now.

Before I can answer, her two sisters spring into view and demand my attention. I stare at them without looking away while I load random kitchen items into the basket. I'm sure it all has to go into the RV anyway. The words in my head feel similarly random and I stumble over my thoughts.

Kendra gives me a knowing glance and then steps between me and our children to shoo them off. She waves her hands in the air and stomps towards them. "Girls, go pack your suitcases with the clothes we talked about! And books! And grab some games from the hall closet. Go! Before I get you!"

The girls giggle and scurry away from Kendra back to their rooms. She gives me one more look, and I nod back at her and mouth the words *thank you*. She follows the girls to their room and I hear them cheer about leaving earlier than planned.

Aren't I supposed to carry my wife and my children out of burning buildings, across flooded streets, and shield them from pain? Isn't that what I'm supposed to do? How can I protect them when I'm powerless to keep the phantoms away?

Your father is going to die!

Six

Kendra and I finish packing the RV in silence. I make repeated trips between the sweltering vehicle and the house while Kendra fills more baskets. The girls are loading tiny suitcases in their rooms.

"I wish we could leave tonight before it gets too late and get as far as we can. I don't want to lose a day. I could drive through the night." I'm thinking out loud, half mumbling to myself. I'm unsure if Kendra can hear me, but she responds from the bedroom.

"It won't be safe to start tonight," she calls out. "We can leave first thing in the morning. You don't want to pull an all-nighter and then see your sick dad while you're so tired you can't even think straight." She joins me in the kitchen. She's still wearing her apron and smells like baked bread. "If we leave early in the morning, I can prepare meals so we don't have to make any stops while you're driving."

She's right.

We spend the rest of the evening finalizing the RV, cleaning the kitchen, and tidying up the rest of the house. After tucking the girls in bed, Kendra and I stand in the hallway and hold each other just outside their bedroom door. We listen to their whispers and giggles for a few minutes. Their childish joy. Their innocence. I don't want to take this from them.

Sleep is difficult. My legs are in the wrong spot no matter where I put them. Every time I turn, I feel the sheets drag against my skin. My pillow won't stay cold. I've flipped it over so many times that I've lost count, and now our dog is snoring.

I don't know how long it takes to finally fall asleep, but when I do, the morning arrives like a scream. I snatch my phone. The alarm pierces the air, and I fumble to silence it. I scroll through my texts and hold my breath. Angie's text is still there. The phone is ice in my hand.

I stare at the vaulted ceiling and finally exhale. My eyes follow the beam that splits the ceiling into two spaces above me. One side catches the morning light streaming into the window. The other is still covered in shadow. Darkness. Tragedy. Death.

I roll out of bed and tap Kendra's arm to wake her. The coffee pot will beep soon, and then this day will begin. If we don't encounter any issues on the road, today will end with me standing face-to-face with my dad.

After a few minutes, Kendra joins me in the kitchen with a stack of folded laundry in her arms.

"Is that all of it?" I ask, pulling two mugs from the cupboard and setting them in front of the coffee pot.

She sets the laundry on the counter and shakes her head. "Well, that's just ours, but I still have to make sure the girls packed enough. They probably didn't."

The coffee machine beeps twice. Kendra grabs her caramel creamer from the fridge and hands it to me. I prep her mug and pour both coffees. Hers, sweet and light. Mine, black as death. I stare at the contrast before handing Kendra's mug to her.

"Hey Kenge, do you remember when we had to drive up to see your grandma before she passed?" The steam from my mug of darkness drifts into my face. I breathe it in.

"I was just thinking about that. I had to go up twice, remember?" she answers between sips.

"Yeah," I reply. "We drove to Montana together when your family thought she was going to pass, and then we had to come back home."

"I was home for about a week, and I had to turn around and fly back up again for her funeral."

"Were we married yet? I don't remember if your grandma was at our wedding."

"No, she passed before that. She met you the Christmas before we got married, but that was it."

I bring the coffee to my lips and stare into the abyss. How often do people travel to meet the dying?

"I wonder if that's going to happen with my dad. I wonder if we'll be up there and… it will take a while."

"Well, if it does, you won't get fired for taking too much time off work like I did," she says.

It's been about fourteen years since Kendra's grandma Ada passed. They had a special relationship. Much closer than the one I have with my dad. When Kendra turned eighteen, she left home and moved in with her grandparents in Billings. For Kendra, it was more than just a grandparent and grandchild relationship. They played games together and talked like friends. Ada was so tender to her, even when Kendra rebelled. She felt like she could tell her grandma anything.

"Yeah. I'm the boss," I answer and consider the differences in the life circumstances. I am a business owner with more freedom than Kendra had as a coffee barista.

I've never had a relationship with my grandparents. Not one that I remember. When I was a toddler, I learned both English and Korean, and my mom tells me that I translated between my Korean grandparents and my dad. I don't remember. I do, however, remember visiting them when I was much older and not being able to communicate with them at all. All of my Korean language was cultured out of me when we moved to the States.

My relationship with my dad's parents is even more distant. I don't remember my grandpa Jack very well, and I have exactly two memories of my grandma Peggy. In the first, I was five. I was curious about the cigarette she was smoking, so she laughed and told me to put it in my mouth and take a deep breath and swallow. I burst into a fit of coughing and gagging, and I couldn't catch my breath. Peggy pointed and laughed. She said I'd probably never smoke because of it. My second memory of her was at my wedding where she confused me with my father the entire time. She passed away shortly after.

"We'll stay as long as it makes sense to stay, Kenge." I try to sound confident, but I have no idea what this means. As long as it makes sense to stay? I don't even know how it makes sense to go. When my dad dies, how do funeral preparations work in this situation? Is this my responsibility? My father is a stranger to me. Will another stranger offer the eulogy?

My empty coffee mug clinks on the tile counter. "Kenge, do you want more?"

"Not yet. I'll have my second cup in the RV for the drive."

"Oh, yeah. That's a good idea."

I can't stop thinking about this imaginary stranger's eulogy and about the life they would describe. I see them talking about all the beautiful things my dad did in life and his impact on the world around him. My dad's friends and neighbors are there, weeping and hugging one another, joined in the shared loss of their loved one. And I see myself and my family there. We are outsiders. The eulogy paints a picture of my father, but I don't recognize the person in this painting. This eulogy for a stranger could be at a funeral for anyone. We don't belong there among the real mourners.

Kendra carries another basket overflowing with hair accessories and appliances into the kitchen. Cords for curlers and hair dryers dangle from the edges. Before she sets the basket down, she nudges me and snaps me out of the cold and lonely funeral ceremony. "Your dad will be glad to see you. He'll want you to stay as long as you can."

I smile at her and nod, but I don't know if she's right. Will he be glad? My dad told Angie he was afraid to tell me he was dying. Is that the same as wanting me to be there?

This nags at me while we finish loading the vehicle over the next hour. Doubts hang in the air between baskets and snacks and the checking of fluids in the RV.

When Kendra finally unloads the last basket into the overhead bin next to my medical kit, we agree to tell the girls about my dad. Kendra stacks the empty baskets and calls the girls close. The three of them rush to the couch. They're staring at me, waiting for the next exciting news.

"Girls, I have to tell you something. It's very sad, ok? Do you remember my dad? Papa Sam?"

They nod.

"Papa Sam has long hair!" Libby, our eleven-year-old, blurts out to remind us. Olivia shushes her younger sister and then sits up like a student at the front of the class in school. She looks quite serious, except for her unbrushed hair and cartoon monkey pajamas.

"That's right, Libby," I reply. How do I bring death into this space of childhood innocence?

"And Papa Sam is a woman," Libby continues. Olivia's eyes widen, and she shoves her hand over Libby's mouth. Charlie, our youngest, says nothing. She looks at Libby and then back at me.

"Yes… that's also right," I say. "Listen, this is important."

I breathe deeply. I've told my daughters about my dad. Or at least a version of the story that their little brains can understand. They know pieces of my dad's life. I've introduced my dad's gender journey as respectfully as I could. But in the same way I don't have a relationship with my grandparents, my daughters have almost no relationship with my dad.

I continue. "Papa Sam smoked cigarettes. A lot of cigarettes. All through life. Do you know what can happen if you do that?"

"Bad breath!" Charlie finally speaks, eager to contribute. She has a wry smile on her eight-year-old face, and both of her older sisters laugh in response.

"Well, yeah, that too, baby. But something worse."

I have to pause to get their attention. I speak slowly to them. "You can get cancer." I pause again. "You can die."

The girls aren't smiling or being silly anymore.

"Girls, Papa Sam is dying. That's the real reason we're leaving early for this trip. We'll still try to have a fun vacation, but we have to stop and visit Papa Sam first. We might stay there for a while."

Until this moment, they thought they were getting ready for a road trip around America, which might as well be around the world. They were expecting adventure and exploration on a summer family vacation. But now I've introduced death to them. But not really death. It's the *threat* of death. Someone is dying, but they are not yet dead.

My girls are quiet. I look at Kendra, and she shrugs at me. When I look back at my girls, I don't see grief in their eyes. It isn't sadness. I'm not sure I can read my own children right now.

"Girls, are you ok? Is there anything you want to ask?"

Olivia answers for her sisters. "We're ok, Dad. But are you ok?" Libby nods in agreement, and the look on her face makes more sense now. It's concern. They're worried about me.

"You look sad, Daddy," Charlie chimes in. Now they're all nodding.

"Girls, I am sad. It might be a sad trip at first, but it won't stay sad. It'll get better. But it'll be a bit sad at first." I hope they believe me. I'm not sure I do.

Kendra and I make eye contact again, and we agree it's time to go.

"Alright then, girls. Is everybody ready? Buckled up?"

"Yeah," the girls answer, but there is a hesitation in their voices. I see them eye one another. They still look concerned. I turn to Kendra and she pats me on the shoulder.

"Let's get going, Josh."

"Yeah. Ok."

I start the engine, but before I put the vehicle into reverse, I pray loudly enough for the girls to hear. "Dear Lord, I pray we have a safe drive, and that Papa Sam stays healthy enough for us to see him, before— "

I interrupt myself. I didn't mention that we might not make it before he dies. I don't want them to worry about that.

"— before too much time passes. I pray that Papa Sam isn't in too much pain, and that we can bring him some joy. Amen."

"Amen," they say in unison.

Amen.

I wonder about prayer. When I speak the words and encourage my kids to do the same, is it just a way of keeping our hopes and desires in constant conversation with God to create a sense of relationship? Or am I trying to get God's attention to help push some supernatural change into the world?

I back the RV out of the driveway and onto the main street that runs through Dinuba, and other prayers come to mind. I pray I can be the father I didn't have. I pray I can be a good husband to my wife. Both of these prayers come from desperation. I don't know what a good father or good husband looks like. All I know is that it doesn't look like my dad.

Within a few minutes, we pass the 'Welcome to Dinuba' sign onto East Mountain View Road. I peek at my driver-door mirror to see our town behind me. "Mountain View" is

ironically named. We've lived here for nearly seven years, and
there's been fewer than a dozen days where the sky has been
clear enough to see the Sierra Nevada mountains. The San
Joaquin Valley is so thick with haze and agriculture dust that
you can't see the foothills just outside of town, much less the
mountain range in the distance.

It wasn't always that way. I've seen old photos of the town
that show the majestic mountains in perfect clarity. They look
close enough to reach out and touch the snow. In those
century-old black-and-white photos, the past look so much
better than the present.

From Dinuba to Highway 99, the rest of Mountain View is
poorly maintained asphalt, flanked by dusty earth and
orchards. Endless orchards. But these aren't lush, beautiful
orchards with soft leaves that brush against your arms. Not like
the trees back home. No, these are Central Valley desert
orchards, where the leaves and branches are gnarled. They're
tough and thirsty. These trees don't want to be alive.

Between rows of trees in the orchards, I spot men in white
hazmat suits injecting nitrogen and phosphorus fertilizer into
the dusty soil and onto the roots. They're trying to keep the
trees productive, and to prevent them from dying naturally. It's
like endless rows of living dry-rot.

"I hate this drive," I tell Kendra. "It looks like death."

"It does right now. But you can't beat the blossoms in the
spring. The blossoms are beautiful."

"You're literally colorblind, Kendra."

"I can see the shapes and the contrast. I can see th
than you can. And I can smell it all better than you can.

I furl my eyebrows and clench my jaw. "I don't even like the
smell of peach blossoms."

A few minutes pass in silence, and I wonder if I've upset
her.

She finally speaks to me again. "You need to call your mom
and let her know."

"Oh, shoot. That's right. I'm sure she already booked her
flight for later this month, but I think she can change the date."
My mom lives in Korea. She typically flies to visit us three
times a year, once for each of my daughters' birthdays. Libby's
birthday is in a couple of weeks.

I make the call and put it on speaker.

"Hey Mom, I just talked to Dad." I hold the phone above
the console between me and Kendra. "Can you fly down early?
Dad is dying."

"What?! Yes, of course. What did he say?!"

"He didn't say much. Just that he's dying and that he's got
maybe a week left. Kendra and I are driving with the girls right
now."

I talk my mom through changing her flight from California to
Oregon and then having her grab a rental car to meet us in
Bend. I ask her if she's ok to drop everything and change her
flight. She says she can, and that of course she would.

After the call, Kendra reaches across the center console and brushes my shoulder. "When was the last time your mom saw your dad?"

"Oh," I reply. I stare ahead at the highway, trying to remember. "I don't really know. She sent him some letters early after they separated, and I think she sent him some money at some point after the divorce. That was a long time ago. I don't know if they ever saw each other again after the divorce."

"Is that weird?"

I shrug. "Probably. It's normal to me. It's what I know. But maybe everything about my upbringing was weird. So yeah, I guess so. It's probably weird."

"No, not that. I mean, is it weird that your mom is going to show up now, when she hasn't seen him in forever? That's weird, right?"

I want to answer, but I'm distracted.

"Weird, weird, weird," I repeat out loud.

"What are you doing?"

"We've said that so many times, I think the word is broken for me. It just sounds funny now."

"What? *Weird?*"

"Yeah. Doesn't it sound… weird?"

"Ok, Josh." She withdraws her hand and sets it on her lap.

"Fine, fine. Yeah, it might be a little uncomfortable, but different for each of them. I mean, my dad is going to see someone that he left, right? There could be some underlying guilt about that. Maybe seeing my mom will make that surface? I don't know. And then my mom is on the other side. I can't even imagine. Is she still hurt? Is she mad? They've been divorced for so long. For years after the divorce, I assumed my mom hoped he'd come around. I know she moved on, but I can't help picturing my mom being hopeful."

"What about you?"

"I don't know."

Is there a word that describes the tiny space between hope and cynicism? A thousand possibilities of this future interaction between my mom and my dying father run through that space, and none of them end happily. But I want them to. I've always wanted them to.

My mind drifts to age sixteen when my parents first separated. I didn't know it was going to happen. My parents didn't warn me.

It's winter break, and Olympia is covered in fresh snow. My parents are leaving in a few minutes to get groceries or something, and they're leaving me alone in this hotel room. The three of us will be flying to Korea in the morning and starting a new life there, but all I can think about is the life that's ending here in Washington. Nearly everything I own is packed up into boxes to be shipped to our new home in a few weeks. Maybe a month. I convinced my parents to let me keep my Super Nintendo in my carry-on luggage. That way, I have something fun to do between now and when my stuff arrives in Korea.

Once my parents leave, I rush over to the hotel room TV and struggle to pull it forward away from the wall. I turn the TV just enough to barely see the familiar yellow, red, and white ports that connect to the Super Nintendo.

"Yes!" I cheer to myself. I'm dying to play my new game. It's *Final Fantasy 3,* the first video game I bought with my own allowance. The previous game in the series was so good that I can't wait to meet the new characters and explore an entirely new world. I plug the power cord into the Super Nintendo, connect the A/V cables to the TV, and then I slam the game cartridge into the console. A teeth-clenched grin spreads across my face as I press the power switch forward.

My eyes are fixed on the tiny hotel TV screen. I'm greeted by a crescendo of 16-bit digital organ music, growing and swelling in masterful tension. The screen lights up with flashes of lightning behind thick, billowing clouds, and the game's title fills the screen with flaming letters. My palms grip the controller, and I run my thumbs lightly over the smooth buttons. I can feel my heart pounding. I've been waiting for this for so long.

The scene camera pans down from the dark clouds and letters. The screen shows the faint lights of a city built into a glacier cliff. The music slows, and the game's introduction begins.

Long ago, the War of the Magi reduced the world to a scorched wasteland, and magic simply ceased to exist…

It's snowing on the screen and outside the hotel window. We're moving away from my school. My friends. My home. My parents fight constantly, and my dad thinks he's supposed to be a woman. We're moving across the planet so my parents can work out my dad's issues without the judgment of friends and people at church. My childhood is over. *The magic has simply ceased to exist.*

A pothole in the road rattles me back into the RV. The tiny front wheels feel everything on the highway.

In the rearview mirror, I see my daughters laughing together on the large bed, bouncing with every pothole and bump. I tilt my head to hear their words, but the road noise and rumble of the engine drown out the sound. I can only hear muffled voices speaking the incantations of their spells. It's the magic of daughters, sisters, and childish wonder. The rear of the RV twinkles with fairy dust. The streaks of purple and pink on the walls cast a glow throughout the vehicle. The magic of the 1990s collides with the life force of these three sorceresses.

Kendra looks back and chuckles, and then I catch her looking at me. I don't say anything for a moment. Without looking at her, I silently mouth the words, "I love you, too."

She reaches across the center console and touches my arm.

I'm sixteen again.

We're at the airport departures area. My dad is unloading our luggage from the Toyota van. After he grabs my suitcase and sets it down, he hugs me and whispers something while he clings to me. His breath smells like rotting cigarettes.

"I'm not going to Korea with you, Joshua," he says. I think he's crying. "It'll just be you and your mom. I'll follow later."

"Ok, Dad." The muscles in my neck tense up, and I shrug him off of me. *I don't care. I hope you don't follow us.*

I sling my backpack over my shoulder, dragging my suitcase next to my mom. I watch my dad get back into the van. I turn away from him and stare intently at nothing in particular beyond the glass of the airport exterior. I don't want to know if he's still looking in our direction. *I don't care.*

For the next year, while living in Korea, I replay this memory. I watch my dad pull the luggage from the van. I see my backpack placed in my arms. He hugs me, but he smells like cigarettes and I just want to get away from him.

Another pothole brings me back.

I wonder about my mom's experience at that moment. This separation was the beginning of my sorrow, but I forgot it was my mom's sorrow as well. She carried the weight of the separation. She watched me turn away from my dad to hide my pain and anger. She knew this would leave the scars of abandonment, rejection, and loneliness. How does a mother have the strength to carry two broken hearts?

I blink through the burning in my eyes. The tears still don't come.

I try to think of something to distract myself from imagining my parents in the same room.

"Hey Kenge, do you remember the box turtle I had as a kid? The one my uncle Randy and my dad picked up off the highway?"

"I think so. But your dad was an only child, like you. He didn't have any siblings."

"What?"

"Your dad didn't have a brother. How can Randy be your uncle?"

"Oh, I guess that's true. Hm." I purse my lips and try to remember. "I guess I don't know exactly how he's related to my dad. Let me think about this. My dad's dad... grandpa Jack. He had a sister, I think. And I think Randy was *her* son."

"So he would be your dad's cousin," she replies.

"So what does that make Randy to me? Not my uncle, then."

"No, not your uncle. He's your first cousin, once removed."

"Are you sure?"

"Yes, I'm sure, Josh."

"Ok. So then... what's a *second* cousin?"

"That would be if your dad's cousin had a kid. They'd—"

"She did! Oh, what was her name? I think my dad's cousin's name was Kathy. Hm. I don't remember her daughter's name."

"Well, whatever her name is, *that* daughter would be your second cousin."

"Huh. So I don't have an *uncle* Randy. I have a first cousin, once-removed Randy."

"Right."

"Interesting." I'm curious if my memory was faulty or if my parents called him Uncle Randy to keep it simple. "Anyway, he found a box turtle on the highway in New Mexico. Oh! Wait!" I interrupt myself. "I have another memory of him besides the turtle. We stopped by the shore of some river, and he had a black dog with him. I remember Randy taking his shirt off and then jumping into the river. After a minute, he walked out of the water, holding this giant fish above his head. Huge. And then he threw it on the shore, and the dog kept barking at it like crazy."

"This sounds made up, Josh."

"What? What do you mean?"

"It doesn't sound real. Are you sure you're remembering correctly?"

I assemble the scene in my head and notice that it's all cartoons and vibrant colors. In my imagination, Randy is ten feet tall. The cigarette in his mouth is somehow still lit after being fully submerged in the raging river. There's circus music in the background. The fish is a rainbow trout made of real rainbows. Kendra might be right.

"Oh. It probably wasn't a river. That doesn't make any sense. Maybe a lake?"

"You really think your dad's cousin jumped into a lake and then walked out with a giant fish above his head?"

"I think so! That's how I remember it!" I laugh, and the fish's rainbows break through the cloud of grief and death. It feels good to smile. "Wait! Maybe that wasn't it. Maybe the dog jumped in the lake and walked out with the fish?"

Now Kendra is laughing. "Ok, that seems a little more real!"

"Yeah, a little bit. The fish seems smaller now, doesn't it?" I'm laughing, too.

"Do you know what else was funny? When Randy found that turtle on the highway, he and my dad were in the front seat of his truck, and Randy was drinking a Coke. The whole time I was in the back seat, I was horrified that he was *drinking and driving*." I make air quotes with my right hand and continue laughing.

For a moment, I forget why we're driving. I lose sight of the darkness.

"Besides him breaking the law, I thought my uncle Randy was amazing. He looked a lot like my dad, but he was bigger. Taller. Larger than life, maybe. I just thought he was so cool. So when Randy found that box turtle on the side of the road and gave it to me, I named it after him. Randy, the box turtle. We smuggled it onto an airplane to bring it back home to Washington. I actually sent the turtle through the x-ray luggage scanner at the airport, and the security missed it."

"Oh. Is that how he died?"

From the corner of my eye, I see Kendra flinch as the words leave her mouth. I don't think she meant to invite the darkness back. She didn't mean to mention death.

"What? Ha! No, that was fine." I swipe at the air with my hand and dispel the shadow. "My turtle lived for months after that. But I'm not entirely sure why he died. It was in the late winter. Maybe the following spring? My dad said my turtle was supposed to hibernate, and that maybe because I didn't really let it sleep in the winter, it screwed up something in its life cycle. So one day, Randy the turtle went to sleep and never woke up."

"You poor thing. Did you feel like it was your fault?"

"No, not at all." I shrug, but then I wonder about it a little more. A friend once told me about the time he accidentally killed his pet gerbil. He held the little rodent in his hands, and then it bit him. In his shock, he squeezed it to death. The guilt haunted him for years. I don't remember feeling any guilt about my turtle.

"No, I didn't think it was my fault. The truth is, I wasn't convinced he was actually dead. We put him in a burial box with some crinkled-up newspaper, and I just sat there, staring at the box. Over the next few minutes, the newspaper would uncrinkle a bit, naturally. But because of the noise, I thought my turtle was moving around inside the box. My dad had to convince me to stop taking the newspaper out to check on the turtle. Even after we buried him, I wanted to dig him back up because I was sure he was still alive."

"Baby, that's really sad. How old were you?"

"I was seven. The thing is, I don't remember being sad about it. I think I convinced myself everything was ok until I forgot about it."

She tilts her head. "So, you never really processed it?"

"I don't know. I was young. Maybe too young to understand? I imagined the turtle sleeping all winter and then digging its way out of the cardboard box in the spring. Maybe it just moved on with its life. I'm sure he's dead *now*. That was over thirty years ago, but I dunno. Maybe he woke up after hibernation."

"Josh. You don't really think— "

"Who knows?"

The sun is still rising, and the orchards cast low shadows across the highway. I drive past a rock near the road shoulder that looks like a turtle shell, and I imagine it's turtle Randy right now, crawling to safety.

I drive past a few mile posts without speaking.

"Wow, look at the sky, Kendra. It looks like it's on fire."

She looks up from her phone and squints into the vibrant hues that stretch across the sky and onto her face. The inside of the RV is aglow in streaks of magenta, but she can't see it until she grabs the colorblind-correcting sunglasses from her head.

She gasps. "Oh my gosh, that's *really* pink."

"Right? It's beautiful. Can you take a picture? I want to document this trip."

"Yeah. I can get some good shots." She takes several photos, lifting and lowering her glasses to view the sky and the pictures on her phone. "It's sad, you know. Your world is so much more colorful than mine."

"That's why I got you those glasses."

"Yeah, but I can't always wear them. They're sunglasses. I can't wear them inside or when it gets dark outside."

I try to imagine what the world looks like to my wife when she's not wearing the glasses. I've played with some online simulators that let you upload images to see how a colorblind person is supposed to see the world, but they aren't perfect. Kendra has tried the websites, and she says they aren't exactly correct. Or at least not for her. I guess everybody's eyes really *are* different. Maybe "pink" is different for everybody, but we've all just agreed with the labels on the crayons.

It's rare for women to be colorblind. For men, it's about 1-in-12, but it's not random. It's inherited. If neither of your parents carried any of the colorblind genes, there's no way for you to inherit colorblindness. Men only need their mothers to be carriers in order to have their vision impaired. For women, both parents have to carry a broken gene in order to have a chance at inheriting it. The math works out to be about 1-in-200. Due to the genetic lottery, both Kendra and her sister are colorblind, while both of her brothers are not.

We inherit some things from our parents that we don't discover until later in life. Like the joints that ache first when heading into the age of arthritis. Or the shape of the crows feet we get around our eyes when we smile in our old age. Or the propensity to get lung cancer if we smoke.

"At least I can see the fruit on the trees before you can," she says, half to herself.

"Yeah, that's true. It's wild how your brain can pick out the shape of the peaches before they ripen and change colors. I can't see the green fruit through the leaves."

"I know. That's what I'm saying."

"It's like Daredevil! He goes blind, and then all of his other senses get heightened. Superhero!" I nod and grin at her.

"That's not real, Josh."

"No, I know. But maybe most blind people can hear better than normal. Better than most. Maybe not superhero-level hearing. Most people distinguish by color, but if your eyes weren't sending enough color information, your brain learned to identify shapes instead."

"I guess." She nods and takes more pictures.

Later this month, field workers will pick fruit from the orchards in the heat of the Central Valley summer. In their baskets, they'll see more than shapes and colors. They'll see their livelihoods, their hopes for their children, their dreams for their future. They'll see life, where I've only been able to see death in the gnarled branches.

"I wonder if your direction sense is better because you're colorblind," I muse.

"That's not because I see differently than you can. That has nothing to do with my eyes."

"But you see a map in your head, right? You can *see* what a home looks like in your head just by looking at a floor plan. I can't do that."

"That's still not really *seeing*, though. It's not my eyes."

"Hm. What do you call it when you can create those images in your head? Hallucinations?"

"Hey! That's not nice!" she shoots back. "I think it's just picturing. Is that... imagination?"

"Yeah, maybe it's imagination. I think for hallucinations, you have to think it's real. It's like you're interacting with something that isn't there, right?"

"The maps in my head are real, though. I interact with them. That's how I navigate."

"Right, but..." I stumble over the difference and wrestle with this imagined or hallucinatory map in my wife's head.

"Oh, wait, I think I remember. You have control over that map. You know it's not physically there. I think for hallucinations, you assume other people can see or hear the same thing, and you'd be confused if they couldn't. You know that the map is only in your head. That's imagination."

"So *knowing* makes the difference?"

"I think so." I'm less sure than I was before we started talking about it. The brain is so strange. We inherit things like colorblindness and the colors of our hair and eyes, but do we inherit the way we view the world as well? Will our girls navigate the world using maps they create in their heads? I hope so. I hope they don't inherit the grief I'm carrying.

I try to picture Kendra's maps in her head and how she navigates with them, but maybe it's like my wife trying to see sunrises and sunsets without her colorblind glasses. We can only see what we can see.

"Josh, have you talked to your dad since we visited him in Portland?"

"No. He's 'liked' a bunch of my Facebook posts, but we haven't talked or anything."

"Does that ever make you sad?"

"Not really. Besides, we talk to your parents all the time. That probably makes up for it," I laugh.

"He really never says anything on Facebook?"

"No, he doesn't comment. He just clicks the 'Like' button and moves on, I guess. He likes Angie's posts, too."

My dad has a small window into my life. Or at least, the parts of my life that I share online. I try to picture what my dad sees. He sees my life from the outside, viewed solely through the lens of my social media activities.

It's an election year, so I've engaged in a fair bit of political banter, but most of my posts are about my projects. Electronics, welding, 3D modeling, and my car. I've been wrenching on this 1971 Datsun 510 for thirteen years, trying to make it into the car of my dreams. Between swapping out the engine multiple times, replacing body panels, upgrading the brakes and rewiring all the electronics, I'm pretty sure I've turned every bolt in that car. I document and photograph just about everything I work on. The online posts are a bit like a journal so I can remember them more accurately.

Leonardo da Vinci kept journals. Lots of them. He scribbled down all of his ideas and marvelous creations. Some people see the scrawlings of a genius. He probably was a genius, but there's something else there. Where others see his completed inventions, I've always been drawn to his far more numerous *incomplete* ideas. Unfinished projects. There is a sense of wonder that I think Leonardo chased. A question would pop up in his head, and he had to chase it down until he could wrestle an answer out of it. His projects were the demonstration of that wrestling.

My projects are a bit like that. Leonardo da Vinci kept stacks of notes of ways to solve the puzzles in his head. I feel that same energy. I feel the same frenetic chasing of all the questions at once; it's like a room filled with millions of butterflies, with only a single net to catch them. There's not enough time in the universe to catch them all.

"Hey Josh?"

"Yeah?" I shake my head and clear the butterflies out of my mind. I forgot I was driving. I check my mirrors to make sure the RV is still within the white lines of my lane.

"Your dad loves you, you know. I think he really likes the

things you post. I'm sure he's proud of you."

"Yeah, probably." I feel my jaw clench involuntarily. I know what I mean when I say I'm proud of my girls. My oldest excels at academics. She's a consistent high achiever in her schoolwork. I'm proud of her. She'll go far in her education and apply that to her future career, whatever that might be. My middle daughter is so emotionally in tune with people, and she pours herself out into caring for others. I'm proud of her. She's going to learn how to navigate relationships and encourage people to grow. My youngest is witty and clever. She's funny, and she's so creative. I'm proud of her. She'll probably take her skills as a masterful negotiator and become a successful attorney.

I talk to my daughters about their accomplishments and their skills. I talk to them about their futures, and how their talents can be sharpened and put to great use. I dream of their success in their adult lives. This is what I mean when I say I'm proud of them.

If my dad is proud of me, I don't know how to believe it. I don't know what it means.

"More than probably, Josh. I think every parent is proud of their kid, especially when they can see something of themselves in them."

"Sure," I say while dismissing her claim.

"No, really. What kind of stuff was your dad into when you were little?"

"When I was little? I don't know. I guess I remember him tinkering on stuff. That's a little bit like me."

"Oh! In that case, your mom must have really loved that," she says, raising her eyebrows at me.

"You mean how my projects sprawl out a little bit?"

"Josh, your projects completely take over. The desk, the dinner table, the living room floor... everywhere! You're worse than the kids sometimes."

"Ok, ok," I laugh. "I thought we were talking about my dad!"

"We are! I'm sure he's proud of your projects," she teases.

I try to remember the first time I saw my dad working on something. I was young. Maybe five or six.

"When I lived in Germany, my dad built me a bicycle from some broken parts that someone threw away. I think he actually went dumpster diving for pieces."

"You've worked on some bicycles, Josh."

"Well, I cut them up and welded them together to make a goat-cart for somebody. That's a little different."

"It's the same thing. Those were bikes you basically got out of a dumpster."

"I guess," I reply, but I disagree with her. "Anyhow, I remember my dad wearing a white t-shirt and his camo army pants. He sat on a white plastic chair in the driveway in front of our apartment. I thought he was building the fastest bike in the world."

I see my dad tightening the wheel hub bolts and spraying the whole bike bright neon orange. Some orange paint is caught in the wind, sparkling and swirling in the air before disappearing. I thought my dad could do anything.

"My dad tinkered on stuff, but he wasn't exactly handy. He didn't work on cars. He didn't even know how to change the oil."

"Oh, that is different from you. You love working on cars."

"Well, I love working on *my* car. I don't want to be a mechanic or anything. But my dad couldn't work on any car. He tried to change the oil once, but he left the oil cap off. Oil sloshed everywhere, and smoke billowed from under the hood. We thought the car caught on fire. I'm pretty sure that was the last time he tried doing anything with the car."

"Do you think he wished he knew more about working on cars?"

"I know my mom wanted him to know more. But I don't know. I used to think everyone wanted to know more about everything. You know, just curious about life, and wanting to know how everything works. But I don't think that's how people really are. Most people have no clue how a microwave works, and that doesn't bother them. Maybe not knowing how to change the oil didn't bother my dad."

"But you said he tinkered on stuff. If not cars, what kind of stuff did he tinker on? That's curiosity about something, right?"

"Yeah, that's true. My dad was into some weird stuff, though. You know I got into computer programming because of him, right?"

"I'm sure you've told me that."

"Probably. He gave me a book to learn how to code, but I really got into programming because I was into those 'Choose Your Own Adventure' books, where you decide which way you want the story to go. Did you ever read those?"

"Not really. I know what they are, but I never read them."

"They were so great! I loved them so much!"

"I can tell, Josh. Your voice just went up an octave," she teases. "And you're talking really fast."

"I can't help it. They were so fun! The first thing I did when I learned how to write code was to write my own 'Choose Your Own Adventure' story game. You'd read a section and then make choices that affect the story, and then from those choices, you'd make other choices. It was so neat to me. And then I figured out how to code random events into the story, adding some fun complexity to the way the story played out."

"This sounds like your dumb Dungeons and Dragons game."

"Haha! Yes! It basically was! I was creating my own version of a role-playing game before I even knew what Dungeons and Dragons was. It was great!"

"If you say so," she sighs. "But what about your dad? Was he into those games, too?"

"No, not at all. My dad was more into science fiction than

fantasy. Actually, I don't think I ever told you this before." I try to hide a nervous smile from my face. "Ok. It's a little embarrassing. My dad... he was actually trying to make a robot. Or an android. Like a *person* robot."

"Um... no. You've never told me anything about a robot." She laughs and looks at me. "Oh, you're serious?"

"Totally serious. When I was in the sixth grade, my dad tried to build a lifelike humanoid robot he named Myra."

I can see the green screen of that Apple 2e computer vividly. I'm sitting at a desk in my childhood home in my dad's office, and my dad is standing behind me.

"HELLO. MY NAME IS MYRA," an electronic monotone voice chirps. A green blinking cursor prompts for the next line of text to read.

"Joshua, isn't that amazing? You try it!" My dad has a smile that spreads across his entire face.

I look back at the screen and point. "Why does it have your name at the top?"

"Hm? Oh, yeah. It says SAM at the top. That stands for 'Software Automatic Mouth.' It's the name of the speech program. Go ahead and type something and the computer will say it back to you."

I scrunch up my face. 'Software Automatic Mouth' is a funny name, and the voice sounds like my old Speak-and-Spell. I hunt for the letters on the keyboard to type a phrase.

The computer speaks. "THIS VOICE SOUNDS FUNNY."

I giggle in response. "Can I type some more, Daddy?"

"Sure. Type all you want," he says.

"I LIKE PIZZA."

"MY NAME IS JOSH."

"I SOUND LIKE A ROBOT." I laugh at the idea of the family computer describing its own voice. I repeat it out loud in the same monotone voice and laugh even more.

My dad pats my head and pulls something from the top desk drawer. It's wood, with rubber bands, metal loops, and several smaller extremities protruding from it. It looks like a skeletal hand with dangling fingers.

"What is that, Daddy?"

"Let me show you." He holds the large wooden piece in his right hand and then gently pulls on the rubber bands with his left. Like a marionette, the fingers curl and then extend, gripping the air and releasing. It moves like a real hand.

"Wow! Can I try?" I spin around in my seat and reach for the hand. My dad rotates the mechanical hand and shows me where to pull the rubber bands.

"I'll hold it, but you can make the fingers move. It's delicate."

I pull the rubber bands slowly, and then I look at my own hand and try to mirror the movements. My eyes trace the lines of the rubber bands and the metal loops, and then to my tendons and joints.

"Is that how real hands work?"

"I think so. I'm going to attach motors to the rubber bands so the fingers can be controlled by a computer program."

"Huh?"

"You know when you were typing on the keyboard, and then the computer spoke the words?"

"Yeah."

"The speaker on the computer is the output. It's just doing what the program told it to do. You can make the computer use other outputs, like a printer or motors."

"So you can make the computer... do things?"

"Yes! You can make the computer move motors, and those motors can wind up the rubber bands and pull. Like this." He makes a whirring sound with his mouth and slowly pulls on one rubber band. As he does this, a finger extends and points at me.

I'm back in the RV, but I can still see the robot hand pointing at me like it was trying to tell me something.

"So, a weird robot voice and robot hand," Kendra says. Her voice is full of suspicion. "How far did your dad get in actually building it?"

"Building robotic parts that could do stuff?" I shake my head. "That was... really it. I mean, he could make the voice say anything, but wiring up motors for each knuckle on the hand was a bit beyond my dad's skill. He didn't own any electrical tools either. We were poor."

"Oh, that's right. That's so weird to think about. My dad had lots of tools."

"Well, yeah. Your dad built houses for a living. I think my dad owned two screwdrivers, a pair of pliers, and a hammer, and that's about it. I don't think he had the technical skills to put everything together, either. I remember asking him how each motor would work, because you'd need one that could rotate the wrist, and another to bend the elbows. The shoulder would be a huge challenge, because you can move your shoulder around in pretty much every direction. You can't do that with just one motor."

I flail my right arm around to show Kendra. She nods.

"Anyhow, I asked my dad how many motors it would take and how he would deal with the shoulder. He just gave me a blank look. He didn't know the answer."

"Did he ever figure it out?"

"No. But he did make a body for his robot. And... a... face." I use my hand and gesture at my own face. "But not like my face. It was a woman's face. He named the robot Myra and put it in a blouse. He gave it a wig, too."

"Ok, that's really creepy," she grimaces. "And your mom didn't want to divorce him right there?"

"You have no idea. And my dad kept it at the desk. Like, in that same desk chair I liked to sit at."

"Oh my gosh, that's really weird. Like uncomfortable weird, Josh."

"It was terrifying. And embarrassing. I couldn't invite friends over anymore because I didn't want anybody to see it. At night, when it was dark outside and my parents weren't home, I wouldn't play any computer games in there. I was scared of it. And my mom hated it."

"Yeah, I don't think I would let you keep a girl robot in the house."

"I don't know if I would call it a 'girl' robot. My dad made the face out of paper mache or something and then he painted it. And then he stuck a ratty blond wig on top. It was like a robot in drag. Does that make it a girl robot?"

"This was when you were eleven?"

"Yeah."

"Oh. So… years before your dad actually came out."

"Yeah," I say slowly. I make quick eye contact with Kendra and then look back at the road.

"Do you think—"

"Oh, whoa. Absolutely," I interrupt. "I don't know why I never thought about that before. I always thought that my dad's gender issues began when I was around fourteen. I thought his failures at work reignited some past wounds from his childhood."

"It seems like it was earlier than that, Josh."

"Right. This thing my dad was trying to accomplish in this robot makes a lot of sense. Myra might have been my dad's attempt at *being*. Or something. He wasn't really trying to build a robot. I think he was trying to recreate himself."

My stomach drops, and my throat tightens. I thought my rebellious teenage years added to my dad's sense of failure. I worked so hard to reimagine my fights with my dad through the lens of normal teenage angst and rebellion, and not something that pushed an otherwise healthy dad over the edge. I had to learn how to stop blaming myself for the abandonment that followed. I spent years fighting against that guilt.

My dad's questions about his own gender and his exploration of himself started much earlier than my teenage years. I was still a child. Maybe my dad didn't see me as another link in the chain of failures in his life. While he was building Myra, he wanted me there. He wanted to show me all the small projects involved in the process. He wanted me to learn to code, and how to wire up electronics like him. He wanted me to thrive in my curiosity and desire to understand the world.

I wipe the first tear from my face, and Kendra touches my arm again. I look back at my daughters in the rearview mirror, and they're still on the bed. Olivia is reading a book to her sisters. All I want is the best life for my girls. I want them to explore their gifts and talents and achieve their goals. Maybe Kendra was right when she said my dad was proud of me. He obviously wanted the same for me.

"Are you going to be ok, Josh?"

I swallow and wipe more tears from my face. "Yeah, I'll be ok."

"Do you have more memories of your dad?" She hands me a tissue and keeps her hand on my arm.

"Not any that hint at my dad's gender identity, no."

"No, I mean any memories. What's the very earliest memory you have of your dad?"

"The very earliest?" I scan the road for anything that could remind me of those earliest years. I see memories through my own eyes for a while, but as I go back in time, they shift.

"Your memories are from your own eyes, right?" I ask.

"What?"

"I mean, yeah, I guess that sounds weird. When you remember your childhood, you see it happening from your own point of view, like looking through a camera, right?"

"Yeah, I guess so," she replies.

"So they're like *real* memories. Most of my early memories are based on pictures, so it's like seeing my life through somebody else's eyes. My earliest memories are my old photos."

"Like that one in our room? Of your dad pushing you on the swing?"

"Yeah, exactly like that. And the one where he's holding me after I stuck my face in the sugar bowl. Are those 'memories?' I don't actually remember either of those events, but I feel like I do because I've seen the photos."

"Hm. Well, you look just like your dad in that picture of you on the swing. You sit the same way. Your forearms and hands are identical."

We have that picture in a framed 5x7 in our room. I see it every day. I've always looked at myself in the photo, but that's because the sunlight draws your eyes to the toddler on the swing. It's so bright, I'm nearly washed out, but my face is clearly beaming. I'm two years old. Maybe three. I'm wearing a striped shirt, burgundy shorts, and socks pulled up to my knees. I'm too short to reach the ground with my feet. I'm staring at my dad on the swing next to me.

I've always envisioned the picture being about me. But when I think about how my dad is positioned in the frame, and how he's smiling back at me from the shadow on a swing next to me, maybe it's really a photo about a father loving his son.

"I think my first true memory with my dad is when we saw E.T. in the theater. I remember wearing an E.T. shirt. It was green. And I remember crying because the movie was over and I wanted to stay in the theater to watch it again. My dad was carrying me."

"Oh, that's cute! How old were you?"

"I was four, I think. I don't remember much else about that, though."

"Ok. What's your next memory?"

"I think the bike memory is pretty close to that one. And I remember one year when I got a cowboy set with a hat and cap gun, plus a pair of those horseshoe-shaped magnets. But that's really it from my childhood, I think. I honestly have maybe four or five memories from when I was a kid. Seriously."

"It's so sad to me that you don't remember more, Josh. My siblings and I remember everything that happened, and we talk about it every time we're together."

"I think having siblings has something to do with that, Kenge."

"What do you mean?"

"Did I ever tell you about that article with Natalie Portman? She talks about being an only child, and how she doesn't have a lot of memories of her childhood. She said if you have someone you can keep repeating stories to, it locks those memories in your mind better."

Kendra nods. "I think that's right. My brothers and sister and I literally tell the same stories every time we're together."

"Like your dad bouncing around the mall in his new shoes, saying he was *Tigger*? And the four of you siblings getting lost in the woods?"

She bursts out laughing. "Yes!"

"Right, so you tell the story over and over, and it makes you remember it. I've heard you guys talking about it so often that I've memorized it. I feel like I was there!"

"That makes sense. And because you're an only child, you don't get to do that. That's really sad, Josh."

"Well, there's another study on memory that I heard on Radio Lab. They said that you don't actually recall a memory when you retell it. You actually *recreate* it. It's like you're making a new memory each time, and it overwrites the old memory. That can be a problem."

"But it's the same story each time. Why would that be a problem?"

"They said it's not really the same story. When you remember something from the past, your brain can't help but add in new details to fill in the gaps. Like, if there was a duck in your memory of getting lost in the woods with your siblings, maybe you didn't know what kind of duck it was because you were young. But later in life, you might become more familiar with different duck species, so when you recall the old memory with the duck, your brain overwrites the old vague duck with a new specific duck you can easily identify."

"But that means you're not really remembering."

"Right. You're recreating. Maybe that's what memory is. In fact, they said that if you recall a memory you haven't thought about in a long time, the old memory is a more accurate recall than a memory you repeatedly reconstruct. The old memories aren't as corrupted with new information."

"I don't know, Josh. That doesn't sound right."

"I don't know how it works. I don't... remember!" I turn my head and share a wide toothy grin. She doesn't seem amused. "But seriously, I don't remember if the study said that we're only filling in details that weren't there or if we could completely edit details without realizing it. Like swapping people in and out of memories and stuff. I don't know how that works."

"I feel like I'm remembering my stories correctly, though," she replies. "I tell the exact same story every time. It's not like the story changes. Otherwise, my siblings and I would always have to correct each other."

"Hm. That's true. I don't know."

"Yeah, I think Natalie Portman is more correct than your Radio Lab show, Josh."

"You might be right."

I check the mirror to see my daughters sleeping on the bed. It's too warm for them to be under the covers, so they're sprawled out with their arms and legs crisscrossing each other. The rumble of the RV has lulled them into slumber.

My daughters often tell stories and repeat events from the past. Maybe they're locking in memories they'll carry forward into adulthood. Perhaps they'll recreate the stories and bring them into deeper meaning as they get older.

"Oh, I do have one more important memory. I was playing in the snow in the Steilacoom apartments."

"How old were you?"

"Somewhere between second and fourth grade, I think. Anyhow, all the kids were outside building snowmen, and one of the neighbors built this massive igloo. It was so big you could walk inside of it. Not just me as a kid, but adults could walk in."

"Are you sure? This isn't another one of your big fish

memories?"

"No, no. I'm serious. My dad and I walked into the igloo and marveled at how huge it was. It was barely taller than an adult, but as a kid, I could stretch my hands as high as I could and still not touch the ceiling. It was one of the coolest things I had ever seen."

"Is that why you always build igloos when it snows instead of snowmen?"

"Yeah. That's stuck in my brain forever. Every winter, if there's enough snow, I build igloos and giant snow turtles. Snowmen are boring!"

Five

It's raining.

I haven't seen the rain in months. It started drizzling shortly after we got into Oregon, and it hasn't stopped.

Kendra stirs in the passenger seat. She's been asleep for the past hour while curled into a cramped little ball with her legs tucked under her. She stretches her arms up and rubs her neck to break the stiffness. She could lay on the couch behind us, but she insisted on staying next to me to help me stay awake.

"Oh, yuck. It's raining," she says after a long yawn. "Are you ok to keep driving?"

"Yeah, it's fine, hon. I'm not really tired," I lie. After driving for nine hours, my eyelids are so heavy.

Kendra stares blankly at the water-dappled windshield for a moment and then back at me. Her eyebrows are knit together.

"Are you going to turn on your wipers?"

"I will. I like to let it build up a bunch before I use them. It's kind of fun. Watch."

I flip the switch, and the wipers kick over. A sheet of water whooshes off the windshield and runs like a river down the sides of the RV. Her eyebrows remain furled. She sighs loudly.

"I don't like the rain," she says while watching the water stream across the passenger side window. She presses her head against the glass and stares at the low clouds. She wears a pout on her face. "That's the one thing I like about living in California. No rain. Just sun all the time." She exhales loudly again. "This is depressing."

"Well, instead of rain clouds, we have pollution haze. Dinuba has a whole smog season."

She ignores me. "Do you remember when we lived in Lacey, and we'd go for months without seeing the sun? It was so hard to feel excited about anything."

"Yeah. We had nearly a hundred days of rain one year."

"Right? We couldn't do anything or go anywhere. No gardening, no walks. We were cooped up in the house. I had to get into a tanning bed so I wouldn't go crazy. I can't believe it doesn't bother you."

Everyone has a different metaphor for the rain. Driving to see my dying father, I'm sure Kendra would say that rain is sadness. It's tears falling from heaven this afternoon. She'd say the rain is associated with grief and death, hopelessness and dread. I wonder if she suffers from seasonal affective disorder.

I've never viewed the rain negatively, but that might be because I grew up in the Pacific Northwest. You can expect rain to fall every day during the wet season. I don't mind not seeing the sun from December to March. I prefer the rain. It's not a symbol of death or sadness to me. It's the opposite. Rain brings new growth. New life. It washes the dirt away. The world grows green with it.

I flip the wiper switch again. Another river flows across the RV.

Kendra cranes her neck over her seat to look behind us. "The girls are sleeping again. They all crawled back into our bed."

Our daughters have stayed quiet for most of the trip. Between reading together and then eating chips and sandwiches Kendra prepared on the road, they've spoken in hushed tones and have only made quick glances at me through the rearview mirror. I usually sit and talk with them through challenging school projects or obstacles, but I don't know what to say to them about death. Especially the death of an estranged grandfather who identifies as a woman. I don't know how to navigate this, much less try to walk them through it.

"Do you think we should wake them up before we get there, or do you want to let them sleep?" I ask.

"It's ok if they sleep. It's summer."

She yawns again and looks at me with eyes half-shut. "Is it ok if I go back to sleep, Josh? I can't keep my eyes open. You're alright to keep driving? Do you need anything?"

"I'll pull over and park if I need to. I'll be fine, baby."

"Ok," she says with her eyes already closed. She adjusts her position in the seat and leans her head against the window. She drifts back to sleep within minutes, and then it's just me and the rain again.

No, it's not the rain that bothers me. It's that we're heading to the land of death. I force myself to exhale and try to stretch out the tension that's growing in my shoulders. We still have hours ahead of us, and the dread is building. The presence of death has been lingering in these quieter moments, and the phantoms whisper in my ear.

I stare at the dotted lines on the two-lane highway until hypnosis sets in. The parallel white lines on the sides of the highway point forward like arrows to a horizon that ends in foothills. They look like mounds of dirt. Unmarked graves. It's the cemetery of people in my life who've died.

I see a teenage boy in my church youth group. He drowns in the local lake after diving and getting trapped in the aquatic weeds on the lake floor. I see a friend from high school who dies on the surgery table due to a genetic defect, leaving behind a wife and twin toddlers who bear the fiery red hair of their father. I see another friend from high school fall to his knees after someone stabs him in the stomach as part of a gang initiation shortly after graduating. I see a childhood friend who doesn't wake up from anesthesia after a routine medical procedure. I see a friend from high school collapse after sudden heart failure on her front porch.

I grip the steering wheel until my hands ache, and I mutter profanities at God.

The phantoms are no longer whispering. They shriek. *You couldn't stop them from dying. You couldn't help them. You can't help your father.*

My foot presses deep into the gas pedal. The RV roars forward.

I don't understand grief. Of all the ways humans have evolved to deal with stress and cope with difficulty, why does loss break us so much? We've dealt with the loss of loved ones for our entire human existence, but we're still haunted by it. Every time.

The bumps and dips in the Oregon highway rattle through the vehicle, amplified by the increasing speed. The RV suspension begins to creak and shudder with the stress of acceleration. I flip the wiper switch to the maximum setting to match the rush of rain against the windshield.

Maybe we don't know how to deal with death because God never intended it. Death is the opposite of life. It's the opposite of goodness. Maybe experiencing someone else's death is a taste of hell and being apart from God.

The steering wheel jitters in my hands. The small front wheels could burst and shred the RV steering linkages at any moment, causing us to careen off the road and plunge into Klamath Lake.

In the grief, there are moments when we don't care if we

die. That's hopelessness, right? A sense that it doesn't even matter?

I swallow the lump in my throat and let off the gas pedal to give the vehicle a chance to slow down. The RV decelerates just before we enter a winding section of the highway.

Maybe I should find a place to pull over to sleep for a bit.

After fourteen hours of driving through the wilderness, I'm the first of my family to step outside the RV. We're in Bend, Oregon. High desert. A God-forsaken land.

I'm standing on the sidewalk next to the three-story apartment, and the cool rain calms me. It doesn't wash away the ache, but my shoulders release their tension. I can feel a lightness in my neck and back. It feels like fifth grade when I would walk home after school alone. The rain was my constant friend. There is so much life in the blooming, and in the grass, and in the moss. The rain is life. It's the only thing holding back death.

The kids bumble out of the RV after Kendra, and I lock up behind them. We've never been to this part of Oregon, but the rain feels familiar. There's a strange comfort here. The kids run to the apartment entrance to escape the downpour, and Kendra chases after them, covering her head with her purse. I give my parking job a quick glance to make sure the RV isn't sticking out too far, and then I stand still and breathe in the clear air. The rain and the dread of death pour over me like a cocktail of soothing anguish.

I open my eyes and trudge the path to the apartment entrance to join my wife and daughters. There is so much weight in my steps.

There's a theory about how we experience time. During extreme stress, our brains begin taking more snapshots of the events we're experiencing. It feels like the moment is being stretched out through time, so we can almost pause to think about things as they happen. This is tied to people feeling like their lives "flash before their eyes" when they believe they're dying. Maybe this slowing of time allows us to reflect on the past and the decisions that led us to this moment.

I'm walking toward my family, but they aren't getting closer. Every step is molasses. This slowing of time is killing me.

A thousand steps later, I'm standing at the entrance of the three-story building. The apartment wraps around us like a giant concrete serpent coiling around its prey. My girls are huddled together, waiting for me to tell them where to go. I wish I was a child right now. I'd like someone to tell me where to go.

Inside, the apartment lobby feels like a hotel. There's a black concierge desk with two people standing behind it. There is a small sitting room to the right where a Continental breakfast might be served in the morning. Past the desk is a dark elevator door that appears to draw all the available light and oxygen into it like a yawning black hole.

I stare at a placard on the wall that reads "Vintage at Bend Senior Apartment Homes" long enough for the sharply-dressed blond woman behind the desk to respond.

"Hi, can I help you?" Her voice is calm and friendly, entirely in contrast to the tone I expect from the gatekeepers of death. A short, dark-haired man is standing next to her, and he appears to defer to her authority.

I step forward and respond. "We're looking for Sam?"

The two people exchange glances, and the woman shrugs. "I'm terribly sorry, but I'm afraid we don't have anyone here by that name."

I wonder how many tenants live in this apartment and whether she could possibly know everyone who lived here. A 'Senior Apartment Home' is an assisted living home, so there must be a fair amount of turnover. People come to an assisted living home because they are dying, don't they?

But maybe she doesn't know my dad by his birth name. My father gave up that name a long time ago. Before my parents split, I saw documents in a desk drawer where he scribbled the name Samantha on the signature line. Later, I heard him say the name Vera as a possibility. But on the return address on a letter he sent me many years later, I learned the name that he settled on after his surgery.

I close my eyes and force myself to say it. "Anna. Anna Brennan."

"Oh, yes!" They both move with new purpose and energy.

They light up like they were expecting us. "Anna is on the second floor. Will you all be going up?"

"Yes. All of us," I reply through gritted teeth.

My youngest daughter tugs on my pant leg. "Who's Anna?"

I speak loudly enough for the woman behind the counter to hear me. "That's Papa Sam, Charlie."

"Oh," Charlie replies. She stares forward and squints. I don't think she understands.

I look down at Charlie and then back up at the woman behind the counter. "You said the second floor?"

She nods and gestures toward the black hole.

The five of us walk into the elevator, and I can feel the heat and tightness in my neck increase again when the doors close. The elevator shutters and starts the ascent to the second floor. I stare up at the floor indicator and watch to see it switch from 1 to 2, but it doesn't change. I wonder if I'm stuck in time again. Has the world slowed?

I look down at my daughters and see them fidgeting and shuffling. Kendra squeezes my hand, and I look at her and see she's staring at the elevator numbers as well. I'm not stuck in time.

I was afraid of elevators as a child. I was always scared the doors would seal shut and never reopen, leaving me stuck inside while water from some mysterious source would pour into the chamber of death. I don't know what movie I watched that prompted this fear, but it left me scared of any room that didn't have windows to see outside. Elevators, closets with latching doors, and even public restrooms. Once, at an airport, I wedged one of my shoes into the door jam to prevent it from closing, and then I hopped on one foot to the urinal.

I thought I was over that fear, but water pours from a secret spigot in the elevator ceiling. It's slowly filling the elevator with ice-cold water. The buttons are unresponsive, so I have to hold my children up above the rising water to keep them alive. The elevator ceiling has a secret door, but it's only large enough for my wife and daughters to squeeze through and escape. I'm stuck in this watery grave alone.

Alone with the phantoms.

They've whispered to me all afternoon. *Your father is going to die!*

I'm underwater now. My wife and daughters are safe. They're climbing up the steel cables in the elevator shaft above me, and I'm left to hold my breath here until I die. There's no use flailing and struggling. I plug my ears to block out the phantoms, but their voices penetrate water, and blood, and bone. *Your father is going to die!*

This is a very slow elevator.

The doors finally jitter open, and the imaginary waters of my fear pour out on the second-floor carpet. I can't tell if the musty smell of old, damp carpet is real or just in my head. Is the carpet damp? Or is this the smell of looming death?

A placard on the wall in front of us tells us my dad's room is to the left.

The five of us follow the sign, and as I pass the doors of apartments between the elevator and room 211, I wonder how many people are behind them waiting to die. How many people took their final steps in life to walk across this faded and musty red and brown carpet and into their rooms, only to leave on a stretcher covered in a dark sheet? Why is a place like this called an assisted living home when they're really just slowly ushering people into the grave?

We gather in front of room 211 and stand in front of the door.

The door is a plain slab, like a tombstone, with a brushed nickel handle. The door used to be white. Time and lingering cigarette smoke have yellowed the paint in uneven streaks, and the area immediately next to the door handle is stained from the hands of past residents, caretakers, and coroners. There's a tiny peephole in the door. A tiny window into hell itself.

The last time I found myself in hell, my mom called to tell me to wish my dad a happy birthday. He just turned 50. This memory is so vivid I can still feel the churn of confused emotions.

I'm twenty years old. I'm lying on my bed when the phone rings. The caller ID is a jumble of numbers on my old cell phone, which tells me it's my mom calling me from Korea.

"Hi, Joshua. Have you called your dad yet? You need to call him today."

"Ok, hi? Nice to hear from you, too, Mom." I don't often get phone calls from my mom. Most of our conversations are through e-mail. "Why would I call Dad?"

"It's his birthday. He's 50 now."

The big five-zero. That's a lot of years for my stupid dad to be alive. He's had decades to ruin the world around him. Half a century of destruction. Happy birthday? I try to muster up whatever the opposite of 'happy birthday' could be. It's too simple to say *unhappy* birthday. Maybe I wish him an *indifferent* birthday. I don't even care.

"Why the heck would I call him for that?" I protest. My voice is loud, and I feel a heat in my chest. I don't remember the last time I thought about my dad, much less spoke with him. "I don't want to wish him a happy birthday. What do I care?" My hands grow sweaty.

"What? Why are you saying that?"

I sit in silence for a second. My mom's response doesn't make any sense to me. Doesn't she feel the same way I do?

My voice comes out in a shout. "Why would I call him for anything?" I feel the ground shake beneath me. "He was a terrible husband to you and barely a dad to me! I hate him!"

I've never spoken those words before. Not out loud. When locked safely in my head, my feelings might periodically float into consciousness, but they only exist as ethereal wisps of emotion. They're not real. To speak those words out loud is to bring those emotions into being. It allows them to manifest and materialize in a form that can interact with the world outside my thoughts and imagination.

By speaking them, I made them real.

I hear the sound of plastic creaking as my grip tightens around my phone. A stabbing pain shoots through my jaw and down my neck, and I wonder if my clenched teeth are going to shatter like the phone in my hand. The words that left my mouth take shape in front of me, and it's the shape of a man erupting in flames. He's holding my memories of my father in his hands, and each memory is glowing with the heat of an open furnace fueled by an emotion I haven't let myself feel in years.

"I hate him!" I shout again to my mom, and the whole earth shakes. The fiery figure of the man in front of me blazes hotter. Is that me? Is that my father? I can't see past my burning tears, but he's holding one of the glowing memories up for me to see. It's the one of my dad hugging me for the last time at the airport.

This is rage. I am the inferno.

I hate my father. I hate that he left us and never came back for me. I hate that he wasn't around in high school. I hate that I have a transgender dad and have to live with that embarrassment.

The flames burn white-hot now.

I hate that he was able to hurt me.

Despite years of forcing back the pain and convincing

myself that I was fine, the ache of abandonment is still here, eating at me from the inside.

My mom's voice cuts through the roar of the flames.

"How dare you say that about him?" She wants me to be respectful, but why should I be? I wasn't respected. She wasn't respected. She continues. "He was a good husband. He was a good father to you."

"Mom— "

"No, you listen to me right now. Your dad never raised his voice to you. He spent so much time with you, helping you with everything. He loved you so much. And he was very kind to me. He was a good husband, and he did the best he could. He was never unkind to us, Joshua. Never. We're the ones who left. You take back everything you said."

My hand is trembling. I catch my breath long enough to reply. "Fine, Mom. I'll call him. I'll talk to you later."

"You call him right away, ok?"

"I said I will, Mom. Bye."

"Bye."

Tears stream down my face and fall to the ground, but it's me that's falling. I'm tumbling out of hell and into someplace worse. I unclench my fists and throw my phone across the room.

The flames around the memory of my dad hugging me at the airport recede, and the image grows clear. When I shrugged off my dad hugging me at the airport, I think it broke him.

I try to rekindle the fires of my anger, but the flint won't strike. The kindling is soaked with tears. I can't summon anything but grief.

Have I been wrong? Wrong to be angry?

The anger has been eclipsed by the shadow of guilt. I'm so cold.

Was it me that pushed my dad away? Did we abandon him?

I'm in front of the door with my wife and daughters again.

I knock. We wait. And then we hear my dad's faint voice.

"Come in!" His voice is feeble, but it's mixed with a cheeriness that feels like a glowing streak of color across an otherwise bleak canvas of sadness.

I hesitate before I grab the door handle. My dad didn't ask who was knocking. Is this his life, where anyone who knocks can simply come in? Does he know that it's us? Has he simply been waiting alone, hoping that someone would show up? He's so helpless.

It takes all of my strength to open the heaviest door in the world, and when I do, the thick, billowing smoke of death rushes from the door frame and envelopes me and my family. I've been chased by phantoms for the past two days, but my girls flinch this time. This is not my imagination. The heavy, acrid stench of cigarette smoke fills the hallway. Kendra's breath catches in her throat, and she digs into her purse for her inhaler. This monster made of smoke is my father's killer.

For as long as I can remember, my dad smoked. But I also

remember that, as a rule, he never smoked in the car or in the house. I only ever saw him smoke outside or in the garage. My mom wouldn't let him smoke inside. She hated it and complained about it regularly. I saw her smash cigarettes and flush them down the toilet more than once.

The cigarettes got expensive. I heard my parents fighting over the cost, so my dad switched from buying packs of cigarettes to buying tins of loose tobacco leaves that he rolled himself.

During my freshman year in college, my friends and I bought cigars from the local grocery store to celebrate an odd event: all of us were single at the same time. We were all freshly out of relationships and still licking our wounds. My relationship wounds were deep, and I was happy to be in sympathetic company. We drank and smoked our cigars and cheered into the night, and when the celebration ended, I threw myself into bed, face-first. As I inhaled my own breath, the bitter stench of smoke smelled just like my dad. It sickened me. It was so jarring that I vowed never to smoke again. I never did.

My dad never quit.

I let my daughters and Kendra enter the room first, and I don't know if I'm being polite or if I'm a coward for allowing them to face death first. I follow behind them and shut the door, and when the smoke clears, I see the frail figure of my dying father sitting on a little couch with a knit blanket over his knees. The unkindness of the years breaks my heart.

The elderly have always made me uncomfortable for the same reason that infants do. Mortality is frightening, but the frail bookends of a person's life bring me greater discomfort than the thought of death itself. The first few years and the final few years are the boundaries. They're like sentinels standing guard at both borders to remind you that life is only lived between them. Stay far from the edges where someone else has to feed you, clean you, and where you lack the strength to hold your head up. There is barely any life on the frail edges.

My father stretches a skeletal hand into the air to wave us in and beckon us closer to him. He's so much smaller than I remember. He's smaller than my daughters. Skinnier. I study the thinness of his arms, and I can see his bones through his paper skin. Cords of deep blue veins overlap one another across his forearm and up to his fingers. The shape of his skull is visible, and I wince at the sight of his protruding cheekbones. His sunken eyes are bright emeralds that cast the light of a glowing forest against the apartment walls.

The light paralyzes me. Is this *my* forest? Are these my trees? I feel myself drifting into daydream. Ivy wraps around my legs and stair-step moss sprouts from the floor.

I shake my head to stay grounded in the apartment. The inviting hiss of the forest rain turns into the hiss of the nasal cannula on my dad's face. A clear tube runs from his nose to an oxygen tank beside the couch. He's holding a cigarette in one hand. He pulls the cannula away from his face long enough to take another puff.

"I'm so happy… to be able to see you girls," he says between breaths. He's wheezing.

I turn and see pain in Kendra's face. She knows these breaths. She's battled asthma her entire life, and she can feel his difficulty breathing in her own chest. She puffs on her inhaler again.

"Girls, you can say hi," I tell them. I want to reassure them, but I'm also trying to hurry them. I want them to say their hellos and goodbyes so Kendra can leave the room and breathe. My girls wave nervously. Libby is the first to step closer to my dad.

"Hi, Papa Sam." She doesn't hesitate to stretch her hand out to his. When their fingers touch, I see the beginnings of the hurricane forming in the collision of hot and cold air masses. There is lightning and hail between my dying father and my middle daughter who is full of life. Olivia and Charlie follow Libby until they're all standing in front of him. My dad draws them in for a hug, and a swirling vortex opens up in my chest. It's the eye of the hurricane.

I didn't know this storm could rip me to pieces like this. I had no idea these last moments could create new pains of longing and regret. Could I have given my daughters a relationship with my father years ago?

"Girls, I'm so glad you're here," he says while studying my

girls' faces. The green glow cuts through the raging storm like a lighthouse. He smiles through soft tears and strokes each of their tiny hands. "I'm so sorry I couldn't be in your lives more. But I've seen all the pictures your mom and dad shared online, and I've loved watching you grow up. You're all so beautiful."

My whole body quivers, and my teeth chatter in the cold.

My girls nod. They're sniffling now.

"Do you still play with the Barbie house I got for you?"

My girls keep nodding. The giant doll house is a prominent structure in our living room, housing dozens of Barbie dolls, miniature plastic furniture, and My Little Pony dolls and Lego figurines. My dad was poor. The Barbie house cost him a fortune.

I spent so much time wondering if my father really loved me, but I never wondered whether or not my father loved his granddaughters.

When Olivia was born, my mom told me that the love of your grandchild is so different than loving your own child. She said it was deeper. More profound. The ache hurt more, and the hope for the child's future was much stronger. I imagine it feels like seeing further forward in time. I see this hope written on my dad's face, and it calms the storm.

Kendra touches my shoulder. "Josh, maybe it's time?" She's been sipping the air to fight off the smoke.

"Ok, girls, let's get you back to the RV. Kenge, do you want to take them down? I'll finish here and join you downstairs in just a minute."

She nods and silently mouths the words *thank you* to me. The girls linger with my dad for a moment longer before following Kendra to the door. I hear her inhale deeply as they leave the room.

I follow them out the door. "I'll see you in just a bit. I'll be quick."

Kendra puts her hand on my chest. "I'm really sorry, baby. I just can't breathe in there. It's so thick."

"I know. I'm sorry. Do you want me to walk you back to the elevator?"

"No, it's ok. Finish up with your dad. We'll be in the RV. Oh, you have the key."

I rummage through my pocket to grab the keys to the RV and toss them to Kendra. "I'll be down shortly, ok?" I turn back to my dad and close the door behind me.

Now, it's just me, my dad, and the phantoms of death who have followed me from the start of the journey.

My dad coughs. And coughs. The phantoms tug at his body and claw at his throat. His frail frame is wracked and contorted as he struggles to clear his airway. It takes him a while to catch his breath, but when he does, he's hunched over and shaking. I want to do something, but I have no idea how to help. My dad looks up at me and shakes his head.

"Emphysema. It's a hell of a way to go, son," he says while taking another puff of his cigarette. More smoke rushes into my dad's lungs and then back out again. The smoke fills the space between us.

So it's not cancer.

"I'm so sorry dad."

"It's nothing you did. I've been smoking for a long time. It was bound to catch up with me."

"I suppose it doesn't make sense to suggest you quit, huh?"

My dad chuckles and coughs and tries to smile.

"No," he says, taking another drag from his cigarette. "I suppose not."

"I brought the family up in an RV, and we're going to camp at an RV park. There's one pretty close. We can stay for... as long as we need to."

"Oh, good. That's good."

"And I got a hold of Mom. She's going to fly over in the next day or so. We have room in the RV for her, too."

"Ok." He nods.

I wish I knew what he was thinking. Is this a burden for my dad? Does he have his own life and people that he would rather have visiting him? And would it be better if my mom didn't show up?

The forest grows around me again. My dad and I lock eyes and I struggle to even turn my head to pull away. The apartment flickers between lush, glowing green and the stark white apartment walls. The phantoms blip in and out of existence, and the world is a strobe light of life and death.

I shut my eyes and step back, and when I open my eyes, I'm back in the apartment. The smoke is here. The phantoms are here. My dad is here.

"It's been a long day of driving. I need to get the girls settled into the RV so they can get comfortable for the evening. Kendra is gonna need some help getting things set up."

"Oh, sure. That's no problem."

"I'll be back early in the morning, though. What time can I come?"

"Any time, really. My social calendar is pretty clear these days," he jests.

I don't know my dad well enough to know if he regularly makes jokes or if this is how my dad is coping with dying. He smiles and laughs through his coughs. It's not what I expected. I don't know what I expected from someone who's dying.

"Ok. I'll go then. You're going to be ok tonight?" I glance around his apartment at the cardboard boxes and piles of clothes. They're haphazardly strewn around the room, and I wonder who has been arranging them. The boxes look too heavy for my dad to move.

"Yes, I'll be fine. I'm here every night, Joshua. I'll see you tomorrow morning."

Will he? How close are we to the end of this journey? Where does this lead? I'm just following the parallel white lines of the highway that end at the base of the foothills. An unmarked grave.

"Dad? I'm glad I'm able to be here with you."

"Me too, son."

I swallow down the heavy lump that's blocking my throat. "I love you, Dad."

"I love you, Joshua."

The room glows green again. How can the eyes of a dying man be so alive, so vibrant, and usher in so much life while communicating so much death?

"I'll see you tomorrow," I say and turn around. I take a couple of steps, but instead of walking out the door, I turn and look at my dad again. I stare down the phantoms next to him until they shrink into the corners of the room. "Bye, Dad."

"Bye, son."

Outside the room, I stare at the carpet and the neighbors' doors and wonder about the stories behind them. Are any of their stories as painful and difficult as mine? I hear the girls talking, and I'm surprised to see them still standing at the elevator down the hall. They're waiting for the doors to open.

"Hey, girls. The smoke was that bad, huh?"

Olivia's eyes grow wide, and she nods in exaggerated motions. Libby watches her big sister and then holds her nose.

"Josh, I don't know if I can go back in there with you. It's so bad," Kendra says.

"I know. You won't have to. I'm coming back up in the morning, though."

"Yeah, of course. You should spend as much time with your dad as you can."

The elevator doors finally open. Before we head in, I huddle the girls together. "Don't smoke, girls. It's very bad for you."

They all silently nod in agreement.

Once we are inside the elevator, Charlie tugs on my pant leg. "Hey, Daddy?"

"Yes, baby girl. What's up?" I look down at her questioning eyes and run my fingers through her hair.

"Does Papa Sam have boobs?"

Kendra glances at me and grimaces. She and I have talked with the girls about my dad being transgender, but we've never gone into detail about the changes to his body. We always assumed that my dad's long white hair would be enough to give my girls the idea. I've never wanted to think about it beyond that.

I look down at my eight-year-old daughter and put my hand on her shoulder. "Is that what you were trying to see in there?"

"Yeah, but I couldn't see anything." She sounds dejected. Her arms flail down dramatically. She stares at her shoes and kicks at nothing in particular.

"No, I suppose you couldn't. Papa Sam's black sweater and blanket probably made it hard to see."

"Yeah. I really wanted to know."

I've never wanted to know. When I learned that my dad was taking hormone meds, I wished I didn't know. When I learned that he flew to Thailand to have gender reassignment surgery, I wished I didn't know. There's nothing about my dad's gender transition that I've ever wanted to know more about because it caused me so much heartache. It just confirmed the distance between a father and a son he abandoned.

But maybe it wasn't fair to view it that way.

"Well, I can tell you the answer, Charlie."

She looks up at me with wide-eyed eagerness. She's curious about everything. I can see a thousand questions brewing in her mind as she tries to grasp how my dad's world works.

"The answer is yes. Papa Sam has boobs."

"Oh. I wasn't sure. Ok." She nods to herself. The gears in her little brain are turning. She may be satisfied with the answer now, but the answer will create even more questions. I pat her on the head again when the elevator door opens to distract her.

"Let's go eat, girls." The five of us head out through the lobby and back to the RV.

Processing

"Hey, Josh. It's been a while. I'm sorry I've been away for so long. It's good to talk to you again."

"Oh, hey. I haven't talked to you in forever. What's going on?"

"I've been busy. Work, kids, pets. You name it. But I've been meaning to swing by and chat with you. Tell me what's new, and I'll see if I can catch up."

"Ok. Well, for starters, I have some bad news."

"Oh?"

"Yeah. My dad is dying."

"Oh, man. Oh, man. I... what happened? I didn't even know he was sick!"

"I'm not entirely sure. I thought it was lung cancer, but it's emphysema, apparently. He's having a hard time breathing."

"Dude, that sucks. All that smoking finally caught up to him, huh? He was smoking multiple packs per day, wasn't he?"

"Yeah, I'm pretty sure. Makes me glad I stopped. It's weird.

You know, I stopped because I noticed that my breath smelled just like his after smoking. It grossed me out so much."

"Yeah, I know. I know that story. How did you find out about your dad dying, though? You weren't even talking to him."

"My sister, if you'd believe it. She texted me after she found out."

"Angie?! You haven't talked to her in years. She just called to tell you that your dad was dying?"

"Well, she texted me. My dad got a hold of her, and then she let me know. But yeah, it's been a long time. Anyhow, I drove Kendra and the girls up to Oregon. Angie says she'll head this way when she gets some time off work."

"Oh, so you're already there. Have you seen your dad, then?"

"Well, yeah. Obviously."

"So… how is he?"

"Not great. It's just hard for me to process everything right now. I don't really have anyone I can talk to who gets it. I mean, I tell Kendra everything, but I don't think she can really understand how I'm feeling."

"She's got that perfect family, right?"

"Well, I don't know about perfect. But her parents are still alive and still together. They're happy. So yeah, I guess it seems perfect. What a completely different world. At least you understand what I'm going through."

"Yeah, it's true. I understand the whole 'weird is normal; normal is weird' view of the world. I'll tell you, it's crazy that everything is

happening at the same time."

"What is?"

"Well, having to deal with seeing your dad and then having to deal with your dad dying. Those are two weighty things to carry at the same time. I'm sure you'd prefer to deal with those separately."

"Would I? I mean, if my dad wasn't dying, I probably wouldn't have any motivation to be here. My life would be like it was a few days ago before Angie texted me. I've gone through life, forgetting that I even have a dad. But if my dad and I had a great relationship, I wouldn't want to have to deal with him dying, either. I think that would be worse."

"If you had a closer relationship with your dad, you might have seen his death coming from further away. Maybe you'd have more time to prepare emotionally."

"Prepare? Do people get prepared for death? I don't think anyone says, 'Oh yes, I'm finally emotionally ready to deal with my father's death.' "

"Hello…?"

"Yeah, I'm just thinking."

"Oh, I thought you left. What are you thinking about?"

"Well, you might be right. Maybe we don't really prepare for death. People die unexpectedly all the time. Anybody who's actually waiting for someone to die over a long period… maybe they just have to deal with longer-lasting grief. Maybe it just hurts more."

"That's what I'm thinking."

"Well, I'll leave you to it. You've got a hard road ahead of you."

"Gee, thanks."

"I'm not trying to be insensitive."

"I know, I know."

"Are you going to be ok?"

"I have to be. I don't think I have any choice."

"Alright. Well, goodnight. Good luck."

"Goodnight."

Four

It's early Friday morning. I'm sitting at the fold-out table in the RV with the girls. We're eating scrambled eggs and toast from Kendra's homemade bread. Forks are clinking against plates, and nobody is speaking. I look up from my plate to see my daughters grinning at me.

"What's up, girls?" I say between bites.

"Nothing," they say in unison. They burst out laughing together.

It's been a good morning for them. This was their first night sleeping in the RV, and they haven't stopped giggling about it. The two younger girls slept in the fold-out bed that became this table while the oldest slept on the couch. This is a camping trip for them, and they're giddy. It's the adventure they hoped for. It's the adventure I hope I can continue to give them.

"Are you girls going to spend the day with Momma today?"

"Yup, we're going shopping," Olivia says in her matter-of-fact voice. "We're going grocery shopping to keep the camper full because we don't know how long we'll be here." She must have overheard me and Kendra talking about it last night.

"And snacks!" my middle child blurts out, grinning. All three girls start laughing again.

I take another bite of eggs and say a quiet prayer of thanks to God. My daughters are having fun. They don't need to grieve like I am. They aren't trying to pick up the pieces of a broken relationship. They can't see the phantoms, and maybe the phantoms can't see them, either.

When the girls finish eating, Kendra grabs their plates and shoos them to the back of the RV to get dressed. She sits where the girls were eating and reaches her hand across the table. Our fingers intertwine, and I can feel her sympathy through her touch. I slowly spin her wedding ring around her finger.

"Are you ok, Josh?"

"Yeah. I think I should stay at my dad's apartment for the next few nights," I say after I swallow my last bite of toast. "I'd hate to not be there if something... happened." Any night could be my dad's last night on earth. Any one of these meals I'm eating could be the last meal I enjoy while my dad is still alive. I wonder if I'll ever enjoy any meal afterward. I wonder if my dad even enjoys food anymore.

"I was thinking the same thing," she says while picking up bits of food scraps the girls left on the table. She sweeps bread crumbs with the edge of her palm into a pile. "I can bring you food throughout the day. Should I bring something for your dad? Do you think he can eat very much?"

"Yeah, I'm not sure. You know what, though? Can you grab some Bugles from the grocery store? I think my dad would like those "

"What's a Bugle?"

"Bugles. They're like... chips. But they're bugle-shaped. You know, horn-shaped." I raise my hand to my mouth and pretend to play the brass instrument.

She cocks an eyebrow at me. "Josh, I have no idea what you're talking about."

"My dad and I used to eat them all the time when I was little. I'd place the cone-shaped chips on my fingertips and pretend they were claws, and then I'd eat them one by one. They weren't very good, but they were so fun to eat."

I stretch out my fingers like claws in the air at Kendra and snarl with feigned ferocity.

"Ok, little boy, I'll look for Bugles. Do you want anything else from the store?"

"No, I don't think so. I can't think of any other snacks my dad would want."

"I mean for lunch. Do you want anything?"

"Oh, anything is fine. I probably won't be in a mood to eat much. Thanks, though."

"You'll need to eat something. I think you'll feel worse if

you don't."

"Probably. Anything is fine."

"Ok. I'll figure something out." She takes my plate and fork to the sink and then returns to the table.

"Hey, Kenge. You know that sensation of having mixed emotions about something? Like, you want to do one thing, but you also want to do the complete opposite thing?"

"Sure," she answers hesitantly. "Why? Is this about lunch?"

"Oh. No, not that. I'm just thinking about all my feelings right now. And how brains work. I dunno. Maybe it's too early to think about this. Sorry."

"No, it's fine. This sounds like our conversation about memories yesterday. Are you still thinking about that?"

"Not really, but I can see how that sounds the same. But no, this is something different."

"Go ahead," she says through a cautious smile.

"When we have mixed feelings, it's not that we're simply torn about something. We have different pathways in our brains that come to different conclusions. Like, one group of brain pathways concluded that staying with my dad is the right thing to do. I'll benefit from spending time with him in his final days."

"Ok," she nods slowly.

"But another set of pathways in my brain has concluded that I don't even have a relationship with my dad. Putting myself through grief is unnecessary torture. I shouldn't have to do this."

"Josh!" She withdraws her hand and stares at me with wide eyes.

"No, I'm not saying that's how I really feel. But I think… I think we all have these competing thoughts. Ultimately, the feeling that floats to the top is a matter of pathway majority. There are more pathways in our brain coming to one conclusion than the other, so that's what we go with. But we feel conflicted because those other pathways are still there, telling us to go the other direction."

Kendra takes a sip of her coffee through narrowed eyes.

"Think of the brain like a country. Nearly half of this country wants one candidate to win the presidency over the other, so no matter who wins, people will be upset. It's national discontentment. This discontentment is those pathways, or people, that want to go the other direction. If the United States was embodied as one individual person and somebody asked them who they wanted to be the president, this collective person would have conflicted thoughts about it. Even after we vote in a president, this United States person will have to hold their nose at their own decision because half the pathways in their brain wanted it to go the other way."

"Ok, that kind of makes sense. It's like, I want to clean because I enjoy a clean house, but I also don't want to clean because I'm not the one who made the mess."

I set my coffee down and take her hand again. "Are you

telling me you want me to finish the dishes?"

She grins back at me. "No, it's fine, Josh. I'm just teasing you. I don't mind."

"I'll wipe down this table. The kids are such messy eaters. Just hand me a rag, I'll do it."

"Josh, are you trying to avoid going to see your dad?"

Half of the pathways in my brain light up in agreement. I have to force them them to comply with the pathways that know I don't have much time left. I have to be with my dad and work through the awkwardness and discomfort. This isn't about my comfort. It's about him.

"Maybe," I answer in agreement. "Conflicted feelings, right? I'll call a taxi or Uber or whatever."

After about twenty minutes, the dishes are done, and the table is wiped down. I've loaded a backpack with a couple of changes of clothes and some toiletries, and I've kissed the girls goodbye. The Uber arrives to take me to my dad's apartment.

"Baby, I'm heading out now. Are you going to be ok with the girls?"

"Of course, Josh. We'll be fine. I'll miss you, though." She puts her hands on my shoulders and pulls me in for an embrace. I don't want to leave. But I want to leave. Conflicted feelings.

Once I'm in the car, the Uber driver immediately engages in small talk.

"Hi, sir. How are you this morning?" he asks through the

rearview mirror. He looks young. Mid-twenties, short black hair. He has a cleanly trimmed chin-strap beard that barely hides his insecurity.

I want to tell him that I'd prefer to have ten minutes of silence on the drive, but I feel the allure of the empathy of strangers right now - the ephemeral vulnerability you can only have with people you know you'll never see again. I want to pour out my soul and talk about my dad. I want to grieve with someone who will tell me a similar story and how they overcame their pain. I want to find solidarity in the mourning.

Instead, I keep the talk small. I punt the conversation toward the banal and ask the driver his thoughts about the upcoming election. We find common ground in how polarized everything seems. I ask him what being an Uber driver is like and if he's doing it full-time. He's not. He just does this on the side while attending the local community college. I let myself get distracted by the windshield wipers that move without any sense of purpose or fun. I keep the vulnerability at bay for the ten-minute drive and thank him with a tip when I exit the vehicle.

What's the emotionally healthy way to cope right now? Do I look for distraction through meaningless chatter, or do I dive deep into the depths of brokenness inside me? I don't know.

I step inside the lobby and stomp my wet shoes on the entry mat. I draw the woman's attention at the front desk. She's by herself this time, and she recognizes me and smiles. The other gentleman is nowhere to be seen. I consider making small talk with her to delay heading up the second floor, but I can't think of anything to say. I nod at her awkwardly and then walk to the black elevator doors.

The elevator ride is less terrifying this time. Or maybe I've simply resolved to let the terror take me. It's hard to tell. Without the anticipation of a first encounter with my dad, I'm much more aware of the elevator's interior this time. The worn buttons, the black carpet floor, the brushed aluminum walls, the flush-mount lights in the ceiling. I double-check to ensure there's no secret compartment near the ceiling that might flood the space with water.

How many people have taken this elevator to their deaths? Maybe they pressed the button to take them to the correct floor, or perhaps a loved one pressed it for them. At some point, they all went up the elevator for the last time. This place is so full of ghosts.

I exit the elevator and follow the worn path on the carpet to room 211 to stand before my dad's door. This time, it doesn't look large or heavy. But there is still fear here. The thought of sitting and talking to my dad weighs on me, and I feel myself drifting again. Is this door going to bring me back to the past every time?

The wood stove creaks from the heat of a freshly lit fire. I'm lying on the floor, reading the latest Excalibur comic book and waiting for the fire to warm me up. I trace my finger over the drawings while I read the pages. I wish I could draw like this.

I'm a few weeks into my freshman year in high school, just barely fourteen. I've made some new friends at the school, but I've also lost a few due to changes in school district borders.

My parents walk into the room from the hallway. "Joshua, we need to talk to you about something." My dad's voice is somber. His face is sullen. I look at my mom, and her eyes are teary and swollen. This is the first time I've seen them like this. I stare back at my comic book and try to escape into the brightly colored pages.

"You know that I've been away in the evenings lately," my dad starts. He comes and sits on the couch next to me. My mom stands behind him.

"Yeah, for work stuff, right?" I reply, feigning disinterest. "You're home late on Wednesdays, Thursdays, and Fridays. What about it?" I don't look up from my comic book.

After my dad left the military, he got his license to help counsel people with drug and alcohol addiction. I would see my dad's pamphlets on the dinner table sometimes, and I wondered why my dad didn't just get a regular job like everybody else. His hours were so irregular. My mom still had a normal job.

"Some of the evenings are for that, yeah. But there's something else you need to know."

I turn the next page in the book and then look at my parents. My mom is staring at the floor, not saying anything. My dad is making direct eye contact with me, and it seems like he's studying me. It looks like he wants to see my reaction, so I resolve not to react. I hold eye contact until I need to blink, and then I look back at the comic book and try harder to fade into the pages.

My dad continues. "Ever since I was a little boy, I've felt like there was something... different about me."

The words could have appeared on the pages of my comic book. Something different from childhood? Maybe mutant superpowers? All of the characters in my comics received their powers during adolescence. They could fly, or teleport, or had superhuman strength. As adults, they wore costumes to hide their identity. They worked together to protect the world. I try to will myself into the world of my heroes.

"As I grew up, I tried doing everything other men were doing, but it never felt right."

I force my dad's words into the comic book panels. Perhaps my dad is telling me that he's more of a loner and less of a team player. Rather than being part of a group of heroes, like Excalibur, maybe my dad is sharing his stand-alone hero role. Not every superhero is a part of a team. Sometimes, they have to go their separate ways. Is this why my mom looks so sad? Is he about to tell me that they're getting a divorce?

"Even now, after marrying your mom and having you, there's just been something... missing. I spent a lot of time studying to see if there was a medical explanation for what was wrong with me."

I chuckle to myself. I know my dad isn't about to tell me that he's a superhero, but he's basically reading the origin story for every character. I look at my mom, and she's still staring at the floor. She's crying now.

"After looking at all the facts, I believe I was born into the wrong body."

I almost laugh out loud. What does that even mean? How can you be born into the wrong body? This sounds more like one of my dad's weird science-fiction shows than any of my comic books. Quantum Leap or something like that.

"Joshua." He waits until I look up. "Son, I was supposed to have been born a woman."

I fold the cover of the comic book shut, and then I'm thrust back in front of the heavy door to my dad's apartment.

Beyond the door is the story of my dad. He believed he was supposed to have been born a woman, and because of that, everything I know about what it means to be a father, a husband, and a man is overshadowed by questions.

It's hard to think about the answers with these phantoms constantly whispering in my ear.

Your father is going to die.

I knock on the door, and when I hear my dad's voice, I push the door open into uncertainty.

Smoke pours out, but there are no monsters. No terrors. It feels as ordinary as visiting a dying father. The room is smaller than I remember.

The rectangular apartment has a kitchenette at the entrance and a living area occupied mainly by a couch, a spindly-legged coffee table, and an entertainment center with a small TV. Next to the couch is a wheelchair-shaped portable toilet. On the other end of the couch, the room has a sliding glass door to a small balcony and not much of a view. The cardboard boxes are now pressed against the wall, and the piles of clothing are neatly folded and stacked. I wonder who moved them.

A hallway off the entrance leads to a bathroom and a single bedroom, but the portable toilet and the couch bedding tells me that he lives here in this main room. I wonder how long my dad has lived like this. Was he this frail when he arrived?

My dad silently watches me as I walk through the kitchenette. I run my hands along the Formica counter edge, touch the coffee machine, and open and close the microwave door. I picture my dad doing the same things, and I try to act out his life in this tiny space, but then I wonder if a caregiver is doing most of these activities for him.

I open another drawer. I think about the dozens of identical microwaves and coffee machines in the building. The caregivers must go from room to identical room, zapping up the same meals and brewing up the same expiring grounds of Folgers coffee for people who are all similarly dying.

There's a terrarium on the counter, and I notice a yellow and brown tail sticking out from an abalone shell and rock cave.

"Is that a leopard gecko?" I bring my face close to the tank and shield my eyes to reduce the glare from the fluorescent tube lights. The gecko's tail disappears when I tap the terrarium wall.

"Yeah. I've had him for a few months. I had another one before, but it died. We're not sure why."

"What's his name?"

"I named him Deuce since he's the second."

"Yeah," I nod. "That makes sense. So... who's going to take care of your gecko? I mean... later?"

"Steve's been taking care of him each day. I'm going to have him take the gecko. I think Steve really likes Deuce."

"Is Steve the caregiver?"

"Yes, that's right."

"How often does he come?"

"Oh, he's here every day. He gets me coffee, cleans the place, and feeds Deuce."

"Fascinating," I reply, half-listening. I tap the glass again, but the leopard gecko remains hidden.

I meander slowly into the carpeted living room. The floor is dingy. It looks like it holds years of cigarette soot that's settled into the fibers. The walls are mostly bare, except for a large poster next to the rear sliding glass door. I step closer to it and see newspaper article cutouts pinned to it. There are areas circled and highlighted.

I hold in a gasp.

There are thumbtacks with red thread linking circled words with other news clippings. Some circled words include "agenda," "leader," and every number, whether written numerically or spelled out. The crimson threads connect all of them.

The first time I saw something like this was in the movie "Beautiful Mind," with Russell Crowe. The main character, John Nash, is a paranoid schizophrenic. In addition to visual and auditory hallucinations, he makes connections that aren't there. He comes to nonsense conclusions. The poster in the movie is a physical manifestation of his descent into delusion.

My eyes follow the red lines on the poster from thumb tack to thumb tack, zig-zagging between furiously circled words and photos of people I don't know. I can't follow the connections. There's no sense to them.

"It's only crazy if it's not true," he says from the couch. He must have been watching me stare at it for some time.

I've never once considered that my dad might be crazy or that he didn't have a proper grasp on reality. Nothing ever made me wonder about his sanity until now, seeing the poster on the wall. Is he unwell? Does he need medication?

"Yeah, that's true," I reply, stepping back from the poster to break my gaze away from the madness. I face my dad. His green eyes are piercing, and I lose all sense of myself under his gaze. A wave of uncertainty washes over me, flooding me with a question I'm too afraid to ask. Is my dad crazy for seeing things that aren't there, or am I blind for failing to see what he sees?

I've never paid attention to my dad's eyes before. They carry so much gentleness behind what may be the veneer of insanity. Perhaps this is just a part of dying. My dad's body and mind are failing. This apartment looks like it's caving in on itself. Maybe I'm just here to hold up the walls and keep the phantoms away for as long as possible.

"Is there anything I can get for you, Dad? Do you need anything from the kitchen?"

"I'll have a glass of water. The cups are in the cabinet above the microwave. Thank you, Joshua."

Every time my dad says my name, a faint ringing in the air makes the room shimmer. The sound is discordant. It holds bright notes of familiarity mixed with the sorrowful grief of missed years with overtones of guilt and fear. Beneath them is the deep note of looming death. The ringing sends the sweetest ache into my bones.

I pour the water from a pitcher on the counter and carry it carefully to my dad. It's only a few steps between the kitchen and the couch, but the apartment is slowly turning upside down. I'm taking care of my father, who is like an infant now, and he can barely care for himself. I'm beginning to feel guilty for not being here for him during these frail years. Wasn't he supposed to feel guilty for leaving me and my mom? It's all backward. And I will hold his hands and usher him into sleep like a child.

My chest is burning from holding my breath for so long. I hand the water to my dad and then sit on the floor near the couch to keep myself from falling into dizziness and despair. There's no way to explain this inversion of roles to my dad. I don't know how to explain this to anyone.

A book on my dad's coffee table catches my eye. The manila-folder-styled cover features a cartoonish large-eyed alien with a classic flying saucer beaming a yellow light down onto it. There's a red TOP SECRET stamp on the lower left of the cover, adding to the faux seriousness the book is trying to portray.

"Alien Invasion Survival Handbook, huh?" I chuckle while I flip through the pages. There are silly illustrations detailing methods of fighting aliens in hand-to-hand combat and warding off psychic alien attacks. I laugh out loud at a drawing of a man leaping from a flying saucer and the accompanying chapter heading, *How to Survive in the Vacuum of Space*. "Very serious stuff here, Dad."

"It might be. You never know," he says calmly.

"Well, I don't know if this is the right book to address the threat." I turn to a page that shows a man holding an alien paper mask to avoid being noticed by other aliens. "I mean— "

My eyes drift back to the poster on the wall and then back down to the book. I wonder if they're related and if everything inside this one-bedroom apartment for the dying is connected with red threads I can't see. My dad's childhood. My childhood. My three daughters. Threads everywhere and tacked into every moment of our paradoxically connected lives.

"Maybe I'll read through it, Dad. Just in case." I force a chuckle, but I swallow down a growing fear. If Kendra's colorblindness is hereditary, I wonder if my perspective has been colored and textured by the brush strokes of broken DNA strands.

I set the book down and turn towards my dad. "If it's ok with you, I'd like to stay here each night. Kendra and the girls can stay in the RV, but I'd prefer to stay in the apartment with you. If that's ok."

"Yes, of course. I have a bedroom I'm not using that you can sleep in."

"Is it ok if I stay out here in the living room? With you? I'd rather just sleep on the floor here."

My dad slowly smiles and nods. "Of course, Joshua."

What is that smile? I see a father smiling because his son wants to be near him. In one view, he's happy the son wants to be close. In another view, he's happy because he wants to be close to his son. But in a shadowed version of the image, the smile represents pity, and the father knows that the son is grieving the inevitable. And then there's an image scrawled in pitch. The father prefers to be alone, so he smiles to mask his disappointment at the presence of a son he wishes to leave behind. Maybe my dad wants to die alone. Maybe I'm intruding.

There's a knock at the door. My dad glances at the clock and then calls out weakly. "Come in, Steve!" He looks back at me and motions for me to go to the door. "I told him about you."

Why would my dad tell the caregiver about me if he didn't want me here? I shove the image of a disappointed father out of my head and convince myself that my dad wants me in his apartment. When I stand up, a large man opens the door and shoulders his way into the room. He lumbers into the kitchen and does a doubletake when he sees me. "Oh, you're Josh," he mutters under his breath.

"Yes, Steve. This is my son, Joshua."

"Nice to meet you, Joshua," he says without eye contact. He rifles through the kitchen drawers and cabinets and pulls out a collection of cleaning sprays, rags, and a plastic bag full of crickets. He moves from cabinet to cabinet with a limp, and I consider the irony of a caregiver needing care.

"Hi Steve. Nice to meet you," I say back to him. I watch him pull a pair of tweezers from the drawer below the terrarium. "Oh, you're going to feed the gecko?"

"Yeah, I do that first," he mutters again. He slides the lid back on the terrarium and then opens the plastic bag. He reaches into the bag with the tweezers, and after a few attempts, he catches a cricket.

"How many crickets does he eat?"

"Two. Every day."

He's curt. Abrupt. I always imagined caregivers to be more personable. I assumed their whole existence was built around giving comfort and care to patients. Their presence should bring brightness and a healing glow to a room and everyone in it. Their job title literally means "to provide care." Apparently, this is not always the case.

Steve dips the cricket into an open tub of white powder, and then he maneuvers the tweezers into the terrarium. I squint to read 'Reptile Calcium' on the tub. Deuce has popped out from his cave and follows the tweezers with his head.

"Do you have to dip every cricket into the calcium?"

"Yes."

I see a flicker of movement in the tank. My dad's leopard gecko leaps from his cave entrance and snaps at the tweezers, causing Steve to flinch back. He's startled, and he begins breathing heavily. After a moment, he shakes it off and goes for another cricket with the tweezers.

"Fun, huh?" I ask.

"No, I hate this," he replies. His voice is very clear this time.

"Oh," I reply, dragging the vowel out. I glance at my dad to see if he heard Steve, but it doesn't look like he has. "Aren't you going to take the gecko after my dad dies?"

He doesn't answer. He feeds Deuce another cricket and then puts the feeding tools away. He begins washing the dishes in the sink, and I let him get back to his caregiving.

It takes Steve about twenty minutes to finish his daily

routine. His final task involves brewing coffee and bringing it to my dad.

"Is there anything else you need, Anna?" he says loudly enough for my dad to hear. I hear it, too, and I bristle at the sound of it. I will never get used to it.

"No, Steve. Thanks again. See you tomorrow?"

Steve grunts and turns to the door. He leaves without saying anything else.

"He's not the most friendly caregiver in the world, huh?" I ask. I'm defensive for my dad. The idea of a caregiver who does not seem to care is troubling. I want better care for him.

"Well, he's got a lot going on, Joshua. He just found out he's dying.

"What?"

"He was just diagnosed with terminal cancer. I'm not sure how much longer he has. He doesn't really have anybody."

I struggle to find words. What is this place? The dying are giving aid to the dying. Today, Steve goes from room to room to wipe down counters and clean bathrooms. Perhaps tomorrow, he'll find himself in an assisted living home, waiting for someone to care for him. It's a spiral of death.

"But I thought you said Steve was going to take the gecko?"

"I know. I want him to have the option. He's been caring for Deuce for a while, and it seems nice to let him continue."

There's a precarious balance of life and death here that I'm hesitant to disturb. I look back at Deuce's tank and then at my dad, and I decide not to tell him that Steve hates taking care of the gecko.

I sit back down on the floor and unzip my backpack. I brought a yellow legal pad and a pen to write down some of these conversations with my dad. This may be the only way I can capture his last days without forgetting anything.

I've kept a journal for most of my life. It's always been to preserve memories and emotions because I'm terribly forgetful. Writing things down locks them in.

My left hand shakes while holding the pen. Do I want to lock this in? It's difficult to place the tip on the paper. I inhale and exhale slowly. Once the ink starts to flow, I'm afraid it won't stop. Writing this down will cast a stronger spell than speaking my fears out loud. Once written, they'll exist in permanency. Indelible.

I write the word DAD at the top of the page and quickly enclose the word in a box to prevent it from escaping.

"Dad," I say out loud, watching the page to see if anything happens.

"Yes, Joshua?"

I quickly scribble down the next few words.

TRAUMA.

ABUSE.

IDENTITY.

I don't circle them. I need to see where they'll lead me.

"So, we've never really talked about this. I know you had

some stuff happen to you when you were young. I know a little bit about your stepdad," I say while tracing over each of those three words again. I swallow past a jagged lump in my throat before continuing. "And I know you were... raped while hitchhiking across the country. How do you think that affected you and your gender identity?"

I don't look up from my paper, but I see my dad nodding slowly. I grit my teeth. Did I hurt him? Did I just wound a dying man? But I need to know this story. I need to know more about my dad's broken past so I can see how it intersects with mine. I'm holding my breath, and my chest is starting to burn again. I need my dad to help untangle these red threads in our lives.

"I don't think it affected me very much," he says.

My breath escapes my lungs in a spasm of coughs, and I'm deflated. There's a jagged line stretching across the page after the word IDENTITY. I grip my pen tighter and circle the word several times to hold it in place. I draw in another breath.

"Ok, but... everything affects everything, right? You didn't *always* think you should be a woman. There had to be a moment when you decided you didn't want to be a man anymore. What does it even mean to *be a man*, anyway?" I can feel the change in my voice, and I worry I'm pushing too hard. I look at my dad, and we lock eyes. Am I fighting with him?

My dad raises his eyebrows. After an awkward struggle, he inches forward on the couch, and rests his thin hands on his bony knees. He leans forward, and his eyes sparkle. "Being a man? Let me show you. Can I use your notepad?"

His face is so close to mine, and the stench of cigarette smoke is thick from his mouth. The lines on his face look so familiar. He has the same crease between his eyebrows that I do. It's an off-center vertical line that splits our brow into two. I inherited it from him. He inherited it from his father. We share a face.

My dad and I have had very brief conversations about his gender identity in the past when I was still a teenager. I was too young to understand. Too hurt to want to understand. The wounds were still fresh, and I lashed out in my pain then. This, too, feels familiar.

I flip to a new page on the yellow pad and twirl my pen twice in my fingers before handing it to him.

He takes the pad and draws a circle in the middle of the paper, but he leaves a gap at the bottom of the shape, making a very tight horseshoe. Where the two curves of the circle don't touch, he draws an arrowhead on each end.

"Do you see this small gap right here in the circle?" He taps the small empty space between the arrows with the pen's tip.

"Yeah."

"I always thought that I could make those two sides meet. That I could do enough to eventually make the circle whole." He coughs, and the pain from his strained breathing spreads across his face. "But as I got more aware of myself, I saw that, in truth, the entire circle was wrong." He breathes deeply. Slowly. "The circle was impossible to close because it was the wrong circle. It wasn't my circle. That circle is *being a man*. I tried to find identity in manhood, and I couldn't do it." He taps the paper with the pen. "You can't strive to become a man. You are, or you aren't. The brain has to be happy with the body."

He hands me the pad and pen and slumps backward onto the couch. His breaths are shallow, and I can see the strain on his body.

"Rest, Dad. We can talk more later."

He nods and closes his eyes. Within a couple of minutes, he's snoring.

The incomplete circle stares back up at me from the yellow page. I lightly trace the shape with the back of the pen and feel the frustration rising in me. I want to tell my dad that the circle is just a drawing. He drew it. A "true universal circle" that defines what it means to be a man doesn't exist. We don't have to obey that definition. The circle is an ideal that we invented.

I flip my pen over and complete the circle. *There!* I yell in my head. *That's all it takes!* What could be more meaningless than creating an ideal and then concluding that you can't live up to it? I want to scream.

The frustration is fuel. I flip the page over and begin scribbling the thoughts that rush through my mind.

What is a man? Not just the roles, or hair, clothes, etc. Perhaps it's

an attitude. It's how you think. Or common interests with other men.
Are these the things my dad has concluded?

My dad didn't have similar interests with other men. He wasn't into
sports, or cars, or other things he believed "real" men were interested in.
So my question ("What is a man?") isn't a question, as much as it's a
statement that being a man (whatever that means) has nothing to do with
the roles, hair, clothes, or attitude. It has no meaning. And if my dad
had grown up comfortable with the idea that being himself was
legitimately ok, there would have been no need for a transition.

I'm scribbling notes as fast as I can, drawing circles around
important words to gain control over them. My mind is racing.
The words that spill onto the page are the ones I'm afraid to
say to my dad.

My dad could have been himself. He didn't need gender reassignment
surgery. I wish he didn't do it.

Tears well up in my eyes. More than mourning the loss of
my dad, I wish he could have been comfortable with himself. I
wish he didn't have that ache and agony of feeling broken,
misaligned, or that he wasn't good enough. He shouldn't have
had to feel that he had to be different than himself.

An hour or two pass, and I've filled pages with questions
and tears.

My dad is awake now, so we spend some time talking about
nothing. We talk about my business, my car project, and the
welded figurines I've made and sold. It's the smallest of
meaningless talk, and as much as I want to find a place of

vulnerability with my dad, I'm struggling to see through the darkness.

There's a knock at the door, and I can hear my girls giggling on the other side. The sound of laughter drives back the gloom that dwells in the halls. I breathe a silent sigh of relief.

"Come in!" my dad and I say at the same time.

Kendra and the girls clamor into the room. Olivia is holding the bag of Bugle chips above her head with a massive grin.

"Look, Daddy! We found them for Papa Sam!" She runs to me and hands me the bag. I show my dad, who fights back a cough through his laughter.

"Oh my gosh! I always loved those," he says to me and the girls. "Thank you very much!"

Libby joins Olivia with another package. "We found the Nutter Butters, too!" she says.

"My favorites!" My dad looks genuinely delighted. His eyes brighten the room again, and I forget for a moment that he's dying and that this may be the final bag of Bugles and Nutter Butters that he eats. I wonder if they'll ever taste the same to me.

"Did you guys already have lunch, Kenge?" She and Charlie are standing near the open door. I can see Kendra leaning back to breathe cleaner air.

"Yeah, we ate before we got here. There's a Whole Foods right up the street." She hands a bag to Charlie and pushes her towards me.

"Here you go, Daddy. It's your lunch."

I take the white paper bag and open it. There's a container of potato wedges, coleslaw, and a vegetable medley salad. "Did you pick these out for me, Charlie?" I ask with exaggerated enthusiasm.

"No!" she laughs and plops down next to me. "Mommy did."

"Well, thank you for lunch, Kendra. It looks delicious."

"You're welcome, honey. Girls, we should get going." She takes a step back into the hallway to breathe. Charlie gets up and hugs me, and then runs back to Kendra. The other two linger for a moment with my dad, and he holds their hands for a few moments longer before they let go and join Kendra.

"Thank you for stopping by, girls," my dad calls out to them. He blows them kisses and waves, and they do the same.

"Bye, Papa Sam," they say, one after the other. "Bye, Daddy!"

"Well, hang on, I'll walk you guys out. I'll be back in a bit, ok Dad?"

"Ok, Joshua. Bye, girls!"

I walk Kendra and the girls to the elevator, and then I take them outside the apartment to the street. The air is warm and feels nearly like summer. It feels like a whole different world outside the gloom of the apartment.

"Wait, how did you guys get here?"

"We took an Uber. I'm going to take the girl shopping around here. There's a few stores that might be fun."

"Oh, well good. I'm glad you guys can keep yourselves entertained."

"Yeah, we'll be fine, Josh. How about you? Are you doing ok?" She puts her hand on my chest and looks me over.

"I think so. I've been cooped up for a bit, but I'm getting a lot of writing done. I'm trying to document everything. I don't want to forget any of this."

"Ok. We're going to head to Costco. I don't think we'll get anything, but it's nice that there's one close. It should keep the girls occupied for a while."

"I wish I could go with you," I tell her, torn between wanting to spend time with my family and fearing losing precious minutes with my dad.

"I do, too. It's not really fun being a single parent right now."

"Sorry, honey."

"No, it's ok. You need to do this. It's just a little hard. I'm just glad the weather is nice enough to get out of the RV."

I hug and kiss each of the girls and then hold Kendra for a minute before I let them go. "I'll text you tonight, ok?"

"Ok, Josh. Love you."

"Love you too, Kenge."

Back in my dad's apartment, the afternoon continues with show-and-tell. My dad tells me about the knitting he's been doing from old grocery store plastic bags. He's made plastic coasters, pads, and a whole rug out of woven garbage. He's made some money selling these things at local vendor fairs and has a whole box full of other woven creations. I wonder what else I'll inherit from my dad.

While I'm eating lunch, I open the bag of Bugles and Nutter Butters for my dad. He eats a handful and seems to relish them. He looks genuinely delighted, so I'm glad I was able to have Kendra find them.

Within the hour, my dad asks me if I can look away. Confused, I stand and turn around, not quite sure what my dad means. I face the balcony's sliding glass door and look outside at the blue sky and the other side of the wrap-around apartment. I hear my dad struggle and scoot along the couch. Every inch sounds like torture, and I imagine my dad's twig-like arms snapping under the weight of his skeletal body. And then I hear a plastic creaking, and I realize that he's grabbed onto the handles of the wheeled portable toilet. The sound of my dad's effort shatters my heart. I want to help him.

The struggle continues behind me, and I shut my eyes. This is my dad's reality. This is his life, every day. I'm in my dad's world. Not the apartment or the city of Bend, Oregon, but in this horrifying existence of struggle and pain. No amount of green-light magic will hold back the terrors. The sounds and smells of wretchedness that follow rip into my soul.

I weep. I have to open the sliding glass door so I don't vomit.

I stop listening. I stop breathing. I don't know how much time passes before I resume living.

The rest of the evening continues with few words. By some miracle of medical technology, the toilet is self-sealing, and the odor doesn't remain except in my mind.

I sit and write. My dad watches TV from his couch. There's a cool breeze that blows through the open balcony door.

Another couple of hours go by, and my dad is sleeping now. I text Kendra goodnight and reread my last paragraph.

Our definitions of male and female shouldn't involve behavior. Being more 'manly' or more 'feminine' are both ideas rooted in cultural definitions. The notion of 'not being man enough' should not exist. We've put impossible goals in front of people, and then we've shamed them for failing to achieve those goals. The labels are meaningless.

I twirl the pin through my fingers and underline the word *meaningless* twice. I wish I could share this with my dad, but we'll never have this conversation. This trip is for something else. It's for saying goodbye.

It's ten in the evening now. My dad is asleep, but I'm restless. I decide to write some fiction down on paper and let my mind wander somewhere else. It's not exactly the same as writing down my memories, but it's related. Perhaps I'll look back at the fiction one day, and it'll reveal something else about how I'm feeling right now.

Aliens.

I glance at the alien survival book and shake my head. One of the consequences of free-writing a stream of consciousness is that you sometimes end up with silly things on the page. It's interesting to think about how little things slip into our subconscious. Underneath the *Alien* heading, I doodle a little alien head with bulbous eyes and then keep writing.

In the event of an alien invasion, we first need to gather resources to survive the initial attack. Once they've completed phase one of their plan, they'll try to establish a base so they can round us up and collect us and eat us. Once they start, we have to learn how to break through the enemy's defenses and seize control of their technology. This is the only way to survive.

I smirk at my own writing. If there really was alien life that figured out how to get to our planet, maybe they would want to eat us. If I had traveled an extraordinary distance across the expanse of space, I might be a little hungry, too. If I was a hunter, I'd be a little curious if the local animals tasted good. Will humanity's future journey to distant worlds make us the invading aliens that the local species should fear?

I start a new section on my page and wonder what will emerge next.

God is the gardener. He's gonna eat us.

I laugh out loud at this next heading that comes to mind and then quickly look at my dad to make sure I didn't wake him. He doesn't stir. Does all science fiction start out with such odd thoughts? Ignoring my religious filter, I set the pen to page and continue writing.

Some believe that God and the angels in the scriptures are not spiritual beings, but are interstellar beings instead. They are aliens. If aliens plan to eat us (as stated earlier), it may also be true that God and the angels would do the same. We worship because we believe that God is good. But instead, God is simply growing us, like a farmer grows his cattle. Until the last moment, the cattle believe the farmer is good. He cares for them. He tends to them. Meanwhile, the angels await the great feast.

I'm fascinated by this little blurb of writing. Maybe I'll write a story about that later. I'd like to explore this idea and see how many places in the Bible I can pull from to continue to weave this fiction.

Nephilim. The Harvesters.

I underline the strange word a few times. According to the book of Genesis, the Nephilim are the half-breed offspring of human women and fallen angels. These offspring were powerful. Some were mighty men, and some were like monsters, and others grew to be like giants on the earth. I always wished the Bible said more about this because it sounds amazing. It's similar to ancient Greek mythology. Hercules was supposed to be the child of Zeus and the human woman Alcmena. The Gorgons were the offspring of other deities. Cerberus, the three-headed dog beast was the offspring of a giant and a half-woman, half-sea-serpent creature. So much weird breeding. I've always wondered if the stories were rooted in a similar fantastical event. Or perhaps ancient people were enamored by the tales of some single clever storyteller, and these stories became religion.

And then God sent the Harvesters a second time. The first was the age before the great flood when they took on monstrous versions of human likeness. The humans feared and worshiped them, but they rebelled when they learned the Harvester's plans. The second time was during the age of information, where people could learn anything. This time, the Harvesters came as Machinations, revealing themselves through whispers in the computers. As humans soared in their technological advancements, the Harvesters grew even greater in strength until the final reaping. The age of man is at an end. There will be no future harvest.

Well, that's some apocalyptic fiction. It started out creative and whimsical and then got a little dark. And this is where I am, apparently. I originally wanted to think about silly things and problem-solve through entertaining cinematic events. I started out with scenes where I'm the hero, saving the city from a cartoon alien threat. But I drifted into questions about the goodness of God. Here, in this new fiction, I have no control. Everything is turned upside-down. I don't know who to trust. It's fascinating to me. The subconscious doesn't know how to lie.

This has been a heavy day. I didn't know what to expect this morning, but it wasn't this.

My phone buzzes next to me. It's Kendra. *One more kiss, love. Muah. The kids are down. I hope you had a good day with your dad.*

I reply. *Muah! Night, baby.*

A good day with my dad should mean we did something fun together. Maybe we went fishing or wrenched on a car together. "Dad" stuff. It certainly wouldn't mean that I'm watching my dad's life flow away from his deteriorating body. It wouldn't mean I struggled all day trying to make sense of his identity while hoping to reconnect. It wouldn't mean that each day might be the last. It's so hard.

I look down at the last thing I wrote on my yellow notepad and feel the tears welling in my eyes.

There will be no future harvest.

No future harvest. These are the last days. The phantoms whisper me to sleep. *Your father is going to die!*

Denial

"This doesn't even seem real. Two days ago, my life was great. Everything was normal and good. It was perfect. Perfect! I didn't have to think about anything like this."

"Was it perfect? I don't remember it being perfect."

"Of course it was. Absolutely. I had everything going exactly how it was supposed to go. I have an insurance business that basically runs itself. Pattie can run the shop for weeks at a time without me. I get to tinker in my garage and work on my car or whatever else I want to work on. Kendra, the girls, all good and happy. Perfectly good and happy."

"I don't think any of that is true, Josh. But that's fine. You can believe it if you want."

"Tell me one thing that wasn't true about what I just said."

"Are you sure?"

"What do you mean, am I sure?"

"I can tell you the real truth, but this won't be fun."

"Try me. I know my life."

"Alright. Fine. Let's start from the top. Your office can't run itself. You set it up so your team queues you up to finish deals, but they can't close the sales themselves. You haven't trained them to do that."

"I'm pretty sure they could close the deals if I asked them to."

"You always ask them to, but you never teach them how. The last time you went on vacation, how many life insurance policies did they sell?"

"Well... none, but— "

"That's right. Exactly zero. Not so perfect, Josh. You built your insurance agency to be fully dependent on you. You tout yourself as a 'good leader,' but you aren't actually leading your team. You're just standing in front of them. You promised you'd train them so they could eventually become agents themselves, but you're not doing anything to help them get there. You've grown comfortable letting them stay right where they are."

"I'll do it. I can train them. I'll make time to train them. What else?"

"Well, you keep tinkering with that old Datsun 510 and telling everybody you're almost done with it. You're not. You keep starting little side-projects on the car and then decide to go in a different direction, and then you just get more frustrated with it. You're never going to finish the car. How is that making you happy? How is that perfect?"

"Oh my gosh, you don't even understand. I enjoy tinkering. It's a creative exercise. The car is a canvas, and it's like I'm painting. I'm creating. Every artist wants perfection."

"You read that on the Datsun forum. Those aren't even your own

words. The only reason you keep working on that car is because you let it define you. You like being the 'Datsun 510 guy' in your group."

"Whatever. That's— no. I don't want to talk about this anymore. This is stupid."

"Oh? I've got more. You think Kendra and the girls are 'perfectly good and happy?' Let's talk about that."

"I said I don't want to. Knock it off. Seriously, knock it off. I'm done!"

"So let's talk about your dad then."

"No!"

"But that's the whole reason you're here. You are ultimately here to settle things with your dad, and you have a lot of work to do."

"I don't need to settle anything. What are you talking about?"

"Your whole relationship with your dad is defined as 'unfinished business.' You have to settle that, or you're going to carry that unfinished business with you for the rest of your life. You have an opportunity right now."

"You don't know what you're talking about."

"I don't know what I'm talking about? You can't even use your dad's proper pronouns. You keep saying 'he' and 'him' and 'his,' and you know that your dad is a woman now. Not just a cross-dresser, like before. Full transgender, post-operation. Your dad is a woman. Tell me that's not an unresolved issue."

"You know I can't. I just... I can't."

"Just do it. Just say 'she!' "

"I can't! I can't do it! He's just going to have to live with that."

"*You mean die with that.*"

Three

My phone buzzes next to my head. It's not quite six in the morning, and I'm groggy. It takes my eyes a moment to focus on the room around me. Coffee table. Couch. Sliding glass door slightly open to provide some breathable air. I'm in my dad's apartment. He's asleep on the couch. My phone buzzes again. It's my mom.

"Hey mom," I say, just above a whisper.

"Hi, Josh. I just arrived at the airport. I'm renting a car, and I'll drive over there."

"Wait, you mean to Dad's apartment? Is that the address you have?"

"Yes, I already have it. I'll be there in a couple of hours, ok?"

"No, no, hang on," I say while forcing myself up with my elbows. "Let me give you another address. I'm with Dad at the apartment, but Kendra and the girls are at the RV park. Go there, and then you can all come to see Dad together."

"Oh, ok! That's even better."

I grab my wallet to dig through receipts to find the business card for the RV park. After I read the address to her, we say goodbye and I shimmy back into my sleeping bag. The floor is hard and uncomfortable, my body is stiff, and my pillow smells like cigarette smoke. I hope Kendra and the girls are sleeping ok.

It's hard to fall back asleep. When I close my eyes, I see an image of my mom standing in front of my dad in the apartment, towering over him. She's not saying anything or showing any emotions at all. She grows larger and larger, until she fills the entire space. I feel defensive for my dad. I want to protect him from her.

I've never felt this way before. I open my eyes to shake the image out of my head, and I stare at the coffee table legs in front of me. My mom is in a better place in life than my dad. She's become very successful in her career. She owns rental properties and travels the world with her friends. She appears to be thriving. Is she? I haven't lived with her since I was 16 when my parents separated. I don't actually know how she coped with the separation and with my dad's transition.

I wonder how the divorce really affected my mom.

My eyes drift shut again, and now I'm at my high school graduation. The excitement of closing out my senior year of high school has faded with the last stanza of Pomp and Circumstance, and I find myself alone in the crowd of blue-robed graduates being ushered outside.

Through the sea of blue, I see my dad. He's wearing black jeans and an oversized black sweater, and his long, wiry hair is far past his shoulders. Does he look like a woman to anyone? I look around to see if anyone is staring at him. Nobody seems to notice or care, but I can't shake the embarrassment.

My mom stands next to him, and together, they look like ordinary parents waiting for their graduated son to join them. My heart stops. I stand still, not wanting to change anything while other graduates push past me to get to their families. If there was such a thing as a graduation wish, it would be that my dad comes to his senses, my mom moves back to Washington, and the three of us are a family again.

We have Applebee's for dinner after graduation. I've lived with friends since coming home from Korea, so my parents don't know much about my life during my senior year. I tell them about my high school experience and what I hope to accomplish in college. I tell them how I've juggled different part-time jobs and about my church. My parents laugh and smile at my stories. It feels like home.

I'm two bites into a buffalo chicken wing when I notice my mom and dad staring at me. I take another bite and ask them what's wrong. After stumbling over their words, they tell me that they both agreed that my graduation was a convenient time for them to come together to sign documents that finalize their divorce.

I open my eyes in my dad's apartment. I can taste the acrid vinegar of the buffalo wings. They've never tasted quite the same after that.

I've always wondered if either of my parents hoped the other wouldn't sign the divorce papers. I pictured my mom hesitating and hoping they could make the marriage work. I used to imagine her crying at the signing table, her grief falling on the pages like rain while my dad shrugged off her tears. In my version of the story, my mom begs him to try to make the marriage work.

The morning sun streams through the sliding glass door and won't let me sleep anymore. I roll over to my side to block the light, but I hear my dad cough. He's awake. It's eight in the morning now. I should be awake, too.

"Good morning, Dad," I say while unzipping the sleeping bag. "The bathroom is...?" I point to the hallway with the question on my face. He nods, and I force myself to stand up and explore the rest of the apartment.

The hallway walls are bare, and I see my dad's bedroom just past the bathroom. His door is slightly open, revealing more cardboard boxes with clothes heaped on top. Clothes he'll never wear again.

I return from the bathroom and stand in the kitchen to stretch the ache out of my joints. After rocking my whole body from side to side a few times, I rifle through a drawer for a new coffee filter. I set the filter in the coffee machine and grab the half-empty Folgers can. The grounds smell terrible. They smell more like cigarette ash than the rest of the apartment.

"Hey, Dad, the coffee here isn't... great. There's a Starbucks at the Safeway across the street. Can I run down and grab you something?"

"Oh, sure, Joshua. I'll take a mocha!"

I don't know if he can taste much of anything. Maybe the mocha won't taste much different to him than the filtered ash-grounds he's been drinking every day.

"Yeah? You really want one?"

"Yes, that would be really nice," he says, adjusting the blanket over his legs. He lights up a cigarette and sets it on his lips.

"Do you care what size?"

"Just whatever they have. Regular size." He closes his eyes and breathes in the smoke of his first cigarette of the day.

"Ok. I'll be back in a bit."

I step outside the room and look down the hall for the exit sign pointing to the stairs. No more elevators for me. I skip down the stairs and into the lobby and then jog to the front doors of the apartment. Once outside, I draw in a deep breath of clean, refreshing air.

I don't know how long I stand there with my eyes closed, simply breathing. I feel like a wilted plant springing to life or a washed out photo regaining its color. This recharging is bringing me back from the brink of death. I see myself wheeling my dad outside so he can breathe in the fresh air as well. In my minds eye, he's cured of his emphysema and tobacco addiction, and he's a man, and he's my father and he wants to throw a football back and forth with me.

The rain picks up, and I don't have my coat. I wipe a tear from my eyes and run to the Safeway, dodging puddles and parking lot curbs. Once inside, I'm stuck in line for coffee, so I spend the next few minutes studying the people before me. Their problems are smaller than mine. None of them are grieving over their dying, estranged transgender father.

There's a man in his thirties wearing a navy blue suit scrolling through his phone. A young woman in a summer dress holds her young daughter's hand, tugging her away from the cake pops in the glass display. An elderly couple stand close to one other, whispering about something they see outside the store window. I fight the urge to be angry at any of them for their mundane lives. I would swap places in life with them if I could.

The smell of freshly brewed coffee helps clear my head. The people in front of me are just waiting for their coffee. They want to start their day with a little energy boost so they can face their own challenges. I've been drinking from a cup of fury and guilt, and it's bitter. Perhaps I should get myself a coffee, too.

"One grande mocha, hot. One grande Americano, hot. Black."

I dash back to the assisted living home, up the stairs, and into my father's apartment. My dad is on the couch watching TV with a cigarette still on his lips. I wonder how many cigarettes he's smoked while I was out.

"Here you go, Dad. One mocha for you."

"Thank you, Joshua."

My dad snuffs his cigarette into his ashtray and then reaches for the coffee with two shaky hands. I hold onto it until I'm certain he won't drop it. I force back the intrusive thoughts of scalding coffee spilling onto my dad's legs, and my dad crying out in pain.

"You got it?"

"Yeah, I've got it," he says to me.

I sit back down on the floor in front of the couch, and we both sip our Starbucks through a few commercials and a few segments of the Discovery channel.

"Oh, I don't know if I told you," I say to break the silence. "It looks like Mom will be in town today. She's heading to the RV park to meet up with Kendra and the girls, and join us here afterwards. Is that ok? Maybe around lunchtime?"

"Yeah, of course. It'll be good to see her."

My dad has been quiet this morning. Subdued. I wonder if he's not feeling well. I've avoided thinking about my dad's health and about how long he has left. I don't want to ask my dad and make him think about it, but I have questions. Does the silence leave him stuck in his head? How much time did he spend contemplating his own life and death before I got here? But these aren't questions I can ask him. I want him to think about something else. I scramble to find a relevant topic.

"So... Dad, Obama just passed a law about gendered bathrooms a couple of weeks ago. Did you see that?" I blurt out. My eyes grow wide behind my cup of coffee. I had no idea what I would say, but that wasn't it. Is my dad's transgender identity contained in a political debate over bathrooms?

"Oh, I think it's a terrible idea," he replies calmly. Unfazed.

"What?!" I shoot back. "I thought it would make things better. Isn't it better for transgender people?" I sit up and set my coffee on the coffee table. I've spent time in these past few weeks debating with people on this topic, arguing in defense of my own transgender dad. I assumed I was making the world a better place for him. How could he view this so backward?

"No, Joshua. It makes it completely worse."

"What do you mean? How?" I can feel my neck growing hot. I can't believe I'm arguing with my dad about something meant to benefit him.

"Listen, son. You need to understand this. Do you think that a trans woman in Alabama was safe before this federal bathroom law?"

I try to orient my thoughts. Trans woman. Born a man, now a woman... in Alabama. So, like my dad, if my dad was in Alabama. Standing against my dad is a crowd of angry bearded men in overalls and white t-shirts and American flags and shotguns. "Well, no. Of course not."

"And do you think the bathroom law made her any more safe?"

"I —"

"No," he cuts me off. "In fact, every bigot in America just found another reason to hate trans women even more. Here in Bend, I can pee where I need to pee. But people need to be safe everywhere. A federal bathroom law makes it less safe for trans women in Alabama because it makes angry people even more angry. That doesn't help." He says all this without coughing once. "More trans people are going to die, Joshua."

I can't form a thought to respond. I've never considered this, but now I see the crowd of angry men chasing transgender people out of bathrooms and into the streets where they are beaten and killed. The hopeful image I've held of President Obama has blood on his hands.

I finally get the nerve to speak. My voice is shaky. "So what's the solution?"

"It takes time. It has to be done locally. You can't change peoples' anger with federal laws. You have to make it safe for people. The trans population is so vulnerable."

"Yeah," I say. "That makes sense, but how do you know if enough time has passed? How do you know when it's safe?"

"What is the black trans woman, Joshua?"

"What do you mean?"

"Picture a black trans woman. Tell me what you see."

I try to imagine, but I can only see the characterizations I've seen on TV. They're always in prison, or prostituting themselves on city street corners, or hiding drugs. Like my rednecks in Alabama, I only have unfair stereotypes in my head. "I don't really see anything," I lie to my dad. I don't want to admit my ignorance or acknowledge my own bigotry.

"You need to see that she's a minority, twice over. She's black and trans."

"And a woman," I add. "So, times three?"

"Right, sure. So she's even more vulnerable, isn't she? If you want to know if a place is safe for trans people to use whatever bathroom they want, talk to the black trans women. They'll tell you. That's how you can know if enough time has passed."

"So, they're the canary in the coal mine. They die first."

My dad looks at me grimly. "Federal bathroom laws don't help."

I nod and wonder what it would take to undo the stereotypes. What would it take to stop the hatred and fear? Not just *out there* but in my own head as well. I apologize to God for my disdain for people I don't know.

A couple of hours go by with more TV and small talk, and then I hear my daughters stomping and laughing their way to my dad's apartment. I jump up and run to the door to surprise them.

"Hey, girls!" I say after I fling the door open. They're startled and then laugh even more.

"Hi, Daddy!"

I reach my hand out to Kendra and pull her close to me, but she resists and winces at the smell. I've already gotten used to the smoke. I wonder if my lungs are suffering from it.

"Sorry, love." I nod sympathetically and hold her hand instead.

My mom is standing behind Kendra and the girls. I smile and wave, but I don't say anything. I take a few steps back and gesture for her to enter my dad's apartment. She steps forward and peeks in at first, and then comes into the kitchen.

Time grows still.

The light in the apartment seems to dim, save for a glowing green pathway between my parents. Even the phantoms grow silent and retreat to the room's dark corners. My mom and dad stare at each other, and I try to capture this mental picture.

There's a moment in a dream where you experience impossible otherworldliness, where colors, emotions, and time collide and become one sensation. It's a dreaming synesthesia. It feels like it exists in the periphery, just in the far corners of your mind. When you turn and focus on the experience, it evaporates. You fall out of your dream and into dark awakening.

I've dreamed of reconciliation for twenty years. My parents are together in front of me, and I'm so afraid to listen to them speak. I'm so scared it will force me to tumble out of hope. I don't want that despair. I don't want to dispel the dream.

My mom's eyes fill with tears, and her eyebrows knit together and tremble. She shakes her head, and I wonder if it was wise to have her come. It might have been better to tell her later after my dad passed. Now I feel guilty that I've stirred something up, and I wish I had the power to rewind the world back to before I called my mom, before we drove up here, back to the beginning before the heartaches started.

"I'm so sorry, Sam," my mom blurts out. She drops her purse to the floor and rushes to his side.

I blink through the confusion of my mom's words. Why is she apologizing?

"You were always such a blessing to me and my family, to my brothers, paying for Chong Tae's tuition. Did you know he's a commercial pilot now?" She thanks him through tears and strokes my dad's hand.

Now she's looking back at me, nodding and sobbing. "Your dad always said yes to everything I asked. Such an answer to all my prayers." She looks back at him. "You were truly such an answer to prayer, and I thank God for you so much. You were always available for me. You always said yes to me. I'm so sorry."

I fight the urge to look away. I'm standing in the presence of my mom's naked vulnerability, and she's falling to pieces. I wipe tears from my eyes, but I don't understand what's happening. There is a look of compassion on my girls' faces, but they don't understand, either. Kendra holds them closely to keep them from being pulled into the heaviness of the moment.

My attention turns to my dad. His smile hasn't left his face. I thought he would become overwhelmed with emotion and that he would break down under my mom's touch. Isn't that where an apology lives? In that touch? In this intimate and sacred space? But his expression doesn't change. He doesn't say anything.

She continues. "I'm so sorry that I had to leave you. I'm so sorry I didn't have the strength to stay. I'm so sorry. I'm so sorry."

I'm so sorry that I had to leave you. My mom's words reverberate in the room, and something inside me breaks.

Years ago, when my mom told me to call my dad for his birthday and insisted that my dad was a good father to me, I began the process of rewriting the story of my abandonment. I learned to view my dad's life through the lens of a father who tried his very best despite his own brokenness. I discovered what it meant to have grace and to give myself grace for my failings as a father. But for twenty years, I clung to an image of a heartbroken mother, and I would not forgive my dad for that.

The embers of unforgiveness have eaten at me, consuming me from the inside, fueling the flames of repressed anger against my dad. I needed him to fix things, but he didn't.

But my mom is apologizing to my dad. I feel my knees grow

weak beneath me, and the weight of my anger falls to the ground with my mom's tears. And my tears. I don't have to carry this anymore. Perhaps I never did.

Is this what reconciliation feels like?

I wanted them to get back together. But maybe I simply wanted peace. I just wanted the raging fire to stop consuming me and everything else in this whole world. I just wanted to set these heavy emotions down.

I'm engulfed in all the emotions now, surrounded by the final flames of a fire that has raged almost my entire life. I see a child, running in the grass and dancing and cheering in innocence. I see the same child, heartbroken at the loss of all the years they'll lose. I see a child in a room by himself, terrified and clinging desperately to hope.

The burning fire in that woodstove in the Lacey house has finally died. No more flames. Just fading embers. Just enough warmth to remember.

My dad clasps his hands over my mom's, and he smiles. He has tears in his eyes as well.

"It's ok, Joni. It's ok. I'm ok."

There are more tears.

How deep a cut can forgiveness bind?

After an eternity of repair, the sobbing grows quiet. My dad makes nervous eye contact with me, and I think he's ready to be done. My daughters are huddled next to Kendra. They're ready to leave, too.

I put my hand on my mom's shoulder. "Mom, I'm staying with Dad for the rest of the week. I think Kendra and the girls want to go to lunch."

"Oh, yeah. Of course, of course." She wipes her face and finally lets go of my dad's hand. "I'll go with them."

Charlie is standing back with Kendra, and she's on her tip-toes whispering something to her. Kendra nods back at her, and Charlie cautiously approaches my dad. "Papa Sam, do you want something for lunch?"

He wipes a tear from his face and reaches out for her hand. "I'm ok, but your dad might be hungry." He gestures to me. Charlie turns and looks at me.

"Sure, Charlie. Anything. Whatever you guys are getting, I'll probably enjoy."

Charlie shrugs and runs back to Kendra.

After they leave, my dad and I remain quiet. I don't know what my dad is experiencing, but it is euphoria for me. There is a lightness that I want to hold forever. It feels like floating. I'm interrupted by my phone.

Dash, dot dot dash.

It's my sister. The text reads *I'm not going to be able to make it. I'm sorry.* I look at my dad, who is curious about the beeps.

"Morse code?" His eyes are inquisitive. "That's the letter X, isn't it?"

"Oh, yeah. It's... it's just my text notifications. I just use different letters for the different apps on my phone. You know

Morse code?"

"I remember a few of the letters. The X stands out."

I don't know if my dad's knowledge of Morse code stems from his military experience or if it's just something that interests him. I never learned Morse code, but it feels like I've stumbled onto a secret about my dad. It's like a secret language between people who understand something deep about one another. But then I remember it's too late to learn a secret language with my dad. There isn't enough time.

"It's a text from Angie. She says she can't make it." I don't know why she can't make it, so I make up a reason. "She can't get off work."

"Oh, that's too bad."

I study my dad's face for any sign of disappointment. I can't tell. I thought my dad wanted her to be here, so I'm upset for his sake, but I can't deny my feeling of relief. I have so many questions for my dad that I know I can't ask if anyone else is around. I text Angie back. *I understand. Love you.*

"I guess it's just the two of us then, huh? Is that ok, Dad?"

"Yes, of course. It's fine."

I still can't tell.

I set the phone down and grab my notepad from the coffee table.

"So, Dad, I want to know more about your story. I want to write down as much as I can." I write today's date at the top of the page and then "Dad's Story" in large letters. I draw a box around the words and look up to see my dad's green eyes piercing into me.

"Ok, Joshua. What do you want to know?"

What do I want to know? I stare at the yellow page and at the words I've written. *Dad's Story.* What is my dad's story? How did he get here? I want to know what happened after he left. Or after we left. I want to know everything. "Can you tell me what happened after you and Mom split?"

"Ok. I can start there…" He trails off, and I can't tell if he's thinking or distracted, but then he nods and pats his knees and coughs to clear his throat. "Ok, I'll tell you something. I wish I had been more mentally and emotionally stable. I didn't have confidence in what I was able to do. I never felt sure of myself. Even when you were young."

I write down *Wished he was more mentally/emotionally stable* and underline it, and then underneath those words I write *(Is this an apology to me?)*

"For the most part, your mom and I hoped to raise you better than we were, but I don't know if we were equipped to do it." He speaks slowly to avoid coughing. I scribble down the words as quickly as I can. "But for the most part, your mom… she was nuts. Just nuts."

I purse my lips and glance at the poster board on my dad's wall. I sketch it on my paper. I try to match the red threads and crisscross the lines from the corners of the page, scribbling while my dad speaks. My paper begins to look like a glistening spider's web. Where the threads overlap, the layers of blue ink reflect the light coming in through the sliding glass door, and it sparkles.

I write *Sam* in one intersection of lines. I write *Joni* in another. And then, with some hesitation, I write *Josh* in a third. I circle my parents' names, but I leave mine open.

"What do you mean she was nuts?" I write *Nuts* under my mom's name. I know she survived her own father's alcohol-fueled rage when she was a child and that she lived a lot of her teen years in fear, but I never saw the effects of that growing up. Not that I remember, anyway. She was just... Mom.

"She just didn't handle her emotions very well. She freaked out all the time. Over everything. Anything, really. And she was so co-dependent."

I draw frenetic squiggles next to my mom's name to indicate her emotional state and continue to write. I write *Relationship?* between the words *Sam* and *Joni* and then sketch lines between the new word and my parents. I've never thought about what my parents' relationship was really like. More words emerge. *Church. Military. Only-child.* Below *Only-child*, I write *Miscarriage* on a drawing of a tombstone to memorialize the older sibling I could have had.

So many words. So many lines connecting them. I feel like I'm falling into the web's threads and I'm struggling to break free.

"But you, Joshua," he says, waiting for me to make eye

contact. He takes a long drag on his cigarette. "You've always seemed so well-adjusted."

I try to write *Well-Adjusted* on my paper, but I can't. The inked lines on my paper stare back at me. They mirror the poster board. Is this paper an account and reflection of my dad's brokenness, or is this my own descent into madness?

The Alien Abduction Survival Handbook on the table reassures me a little. I don't think Aliens exist, do I? I look at the poster on the wall and confirm that I can't make sense of it. Maybe it's just my dad's hallucination. Maybe I am well-adjusted.

"Thanks, Dad. But what about you? What happened after Mom and I went to Korea?"

My dad takes a deep, slow breath and leans back.

"Of all my life's journeys, this was the most difficult part to embark on, son." He takes another slow breath and then pauses. He stares at me with gleaming emerald eyes. "I knew I would lose everyone and everything. But it was the only path if I wanted to keep my sanity."

Sanity? The words and scribbles on my page that represent my dad's world might be anything but sane. It's chaos and brokenness and a tangle of disconnected thoughts. What sanity did my dad think he was keeping?

I flip the page on the notepad, write *Dad* in the middle of the page, and write *SANITY* underneath. My dad continues talking, but I feel a weight on my chest. What is sanity? What does it mean that my dad only had one path if he wanted to keep his sanity?

Under the word *SANITY*, I scribble down other thoughts. *Feeling normal. Surviving. Feeling ok with yourself.* Don't we all seek this? We do what we need to do in order to feel *sane.* To feel normal. To survive.

My father, in a desperate attempt to be ok with himself, stared at the painful reality that he would lose everything and everyone in his life. For my dad, this wasn't choosing one life over another. I thought this was the case. That's why I was so angry. Instead, my dad's circumstances convinced him that the only way he was allowed to live at all was to give up everything he loved and start over.

He's not wrong. There was no way for things to work out. My dad came out in the early 1990s, long before it was socially acceptable to be transgendered. My mom and I couldn't bear the shame. But now I'm more ashamed than ever.

A painful truth starts to sink in. My father didn't reject me and my mother to pursue a better life. My father had to leave because *we rejected him.* We didn't know how *not* to reject him because we couldn't accept him. We left because he wasn't who we wanted him to be. My mother believed she needed a strong, traditional man. He couldn't be one. I believed that I needed a strong, traditional man to be my father. He couldn't be one. So we, along with the rest of the world, reinforced what he already believed: he wasn't good enough. He wasn't a real man, and my dad couldn't bear the failure.

I've lost so much time. Years have been wasted hiding from shame. Decades of anger. I can't wipe away the tears fast enough.

There are teardrops on my paper. I circle each one so I don't forget them.

My dad continues. "When your mom left, I stayed in Olympia for a while. Almost ten years."

My eyes grow wide hearing my dad's words. I write *Ten years!!!* on my paper. My heart sinks. My dad and I were in the same town for a decade and I never once considered reaching out or visiting. I was too angry. For a decade, though? I write *So close, So far away* on my paper. Before I let myself feel too bad, I remember that my dad didn't reach out to me, either. I underline *So far away*.

"Were you at Ron and Trinda's place the whole time?"

"What? How did you know Ron and Trinda? Did you meet them?"

"Well, yeah, Dad. When I moved back to Washington, you and Trinda picked me up from the airport and took me back to their house. You were living there for a bit, right?"

"Yeah…" his voice trails off. His eyes scan the ceiling. He's hunting for the memory, but he can't find it.

"Really, I was there. I slept on the couch for two nights. I remember that you had a possum skull on the woodstove."

"That's right, I did! Do you know where that came from?"

I only have one memory involving my dad and a possum. I was in the sixth grade, and we lived in the Lacey house. We had a little white dog I named *Tinker Bell* because we attached a little bell on her collar that jingled as she ran around. One evening, a possum came into our backyard and got aggressive with Tinker Bell, so my dad pulled out a bow and arrow and shot it several times. I never really knew what happened to it after that.

"Is that the possum you shot with arrows?"

"One and the same. I boiled it down and kept the skull. Like a real hunter!" He laughs awkwardly and nods. "Ok, then. So you *were* at Ron and Trinda's house. Huh. I really don't remember that. But I didn't live there at first. I was in the van for a while before I met them."

"Van?"

"Yeah, our old Toyota. I slept in there for a while."

"You were... homeless, Dad?" I write *Homeless* and sketch a quick boxy vehicle representing our old family van.

"For a while, yeah. I lived in the van. But then I had a friend who had a barn, so I set up a tent and stove in there. It was fine. Fun, actually. Like camping."

A tent. In a barn. Still homeless and vulnerable. A couple of years earlier, my dad was employed and happily married with a wife and a son. He was a homeowner. The only thing missing was a white picket fence.

"How long were you in the barn?"

"About a year. After I met Ron and Trinda, they let me live with them. To pay rent, I got a job at a plant nursery, and then worked as a caregiver. I lived there for about eight years, and then I moved to Portland."

Eight years. Somewhere during that time, my dad went to Thailand to get his gender reassignment surgery. At least, I think that's what my mom told me. I don't really remember exactly when. I've never wanted to know the details.

"So why'd you move?"

"Mainly because Trinda died."

"What? She died? Oh man, what happened?"

"Yeah… one morning, she just didn't wake up. Ron and I were just so broken up about it. I felt like I had to leave."

I write *Ron and Trinda* on my paper, and then I remember something. When Trinda and my dad picked me up from the airport, Trinda told me that she was a lesbian, and she laughed about how her mom told her that it was just a phase, and that she was just doing it to be rebellious. At the time, I thought she was trying to convince me that my dad's identity was like hers. Not a choice, but a real identity. It was simply who my dad was. I remember trying to shut her out of my mind because I still thought my dad *was* making a choice. The wrong choice.

But maybe Trinda was just telling me her own story. Maybe it didn't have anything to do with my dad. Maybe she wasn't trying to convince me of anything.

So what was Ron's deal? I circle his name and Trinda's name together and draw a question mark above it. I always assumed they were married, but if she was a lesbian, I don't know how that works. At the time, I thought my dad was third-wheeling it at their house like an awkward guest renting out a room, but I also have some memories of my dad and Trinda hugging a lot. I remember wondering how Ron felt about that, but... many of these memories don't make sense to me. I write as quickly as possible and hope to figure them out later.

"I really loved Trinda. She and I were so close." I hear my dad sniffle, and I look up to see his eyes are red. I haven't seen him get emotional like this until now. "I loved her so much, Joshua."

I draw a line between my dad and Trinda's name to match the line between my dad and my mom. Then I write *Barbara*, Angie's mom's name, and I draw the same line for her as well. Did my dad love Trinda the way he loved Angie's mother? Or my mom? Was Trinda just the latest woman he loved, or was there something else there?

If Trinda was in a relationship with my dad, and Ron wasn't actually her husband, that would mean that my dad was a trans woman in a lesbian relationship with Trinda. Perhaps this was the first woman who loved my dad for who he really was. Someone who accepted him in his full expression of his identity.

And then my dad lost her, too.

"When I moved to Portland, I took on some odd jobs. I painted houses and worked as a caregiver again. And I met Curtis in Portland. He worked in a convenience store near my apartment. Oh, but before that... before that, I started drinking. A lot. I went to AA for it, actually. After I cleaned up for about a year, I met Curtis."

I never knew that my dad drank. I can't picture it. I've never seen either of my parents drink a single drop. They both just quietly abstained from it. When I was young, I asked my parents about alcohol and whether or not they drank. My dad said he was allergic to it, which was a lie powerful enough to make me wonder if the allergy was hereditary. My mom said it just made her fall asleep. That was the extent of the conversations about alcohol in our house.

Listening to my dad tell me about drinking himself into a stupor or sitting in an AA meeting makes me squirm. I quickly jot down *Drunkenness, AA* and circle them on my notepad, and then draw a line from there to *Trinda's Death* and then another line to *Homelessness.* To *Divorce.* To *Job loss.* I keep writing backward in time through the stories he's told me. *Angie's mom: divorce. Teen years: Sexual assault. Childhood: Abandonment, physical abuse.*

Every story my dad shares is another link in this unbroken chain of heartache.

I draw a stick figure scene for each event. Angie's mom has her kids next to her, telling my dad he can leave if he's not ok with an open relationship. A semi truck at a gas station, and a teenager climbing into the truck, unaware of the danger. A crying child with a black eye all alone on a hill.

I'm suddenly aware that the only thing I can hear is my pen scratching against the notepad. My dad hasn't spoken for a while. I look up to see him staring at me with a gentle smile on his face.

"I'm... just trying to write down everything you're saying," I lie. My page is full of drawings. "It's taking me a bit to get it word for word."

"Ok," he says. "I just want to make sure you're ready."

"Go ahead, Dad."

"It took me about a year to get cleaned up, and that's when I met Curtis. We bonded over our love for camping and wilderness survival. We stayed in Portland for a few years but we couldn't stay there for much longer. A gang moved into the area, and they started getting aggressive about their territory. Violent. Curtis thought it would be better to move to Sun River, so that's where we went. We stayed there until my health problems forced me to move here to Bend. I've been here ever since."

"So that brings us to today, then," I reply. "And here, you lived happily ever after." I write the words down and circle them several times. I want to shut my notebook and end my dad's story here. I imagine a life for my dad with no more heartache. No more betrayals or abusers. Just some peace and quiet.

"Happily ever after," he repeats. There is no sadness in his voice. I want to believe him. I want that to be the story.

"So Joshua, I'm going to tell you something. I think I'm ready to tell you."

I look up from my paper and meet his eyes again. There's something different about them now.

"Yeah?" I ask, searching for hope in his face.

"I'm going to die on Tuesday," he answers.

I don't respond. I heard the words, but I don't understand. I don't want to understand.

"I'm going to tell you a bit about my emphysema. It's important that you know this. It feels like molasses slowly rising in my throat, threatening to cut off my breathing. The coughing is unproductive. It doesn't clear anything out. I'm not strong enough to cough with much force anyway."

As he describes his difficulty breathing, I can't find my breath either. The heat is rising behind my ears. I set my pen down and shut my eyes. I nod back at my dad.

"My food doesn't stay down. I'm constantly throwing it back up, and anything that stays down I void through painful diarrhea. Often. But I don't have the strength to go to the bathroom quickly enough, so I have that toilet chair. It's exhausting to use, and then there's no flushing. I have to wait for the caregiver to come and clean it up and take it away."

I'm drowning in my tears now. I can't breathe.

"My skin is paper. If I do have the strength to move around, my skin rips. My blood oxygen levels are so low that my blood is basically black. It's tar. Joshua, it hurts to breathe. And my circulation is so poor, I'm freezing all the time. I'm in constant pain."

And now I'm falling, and the world is growing dark. Black like my dad's blood.

"I live on this oxygen machine, knowing that I now depend on an external source of oxygen to live. And knowing that caregivers have to care for me until die. I'm just... waiting to die. I'm suffering under the agony of living for several more days, weeks, even months, as the rising tide of thick mucus continues upwards, threatening to drown me in my sleep. Or worse, when I'm awake."

I will my dad to stop. *Please stop. Please, Dad, stop. Please!* I scream inside my head for God to step in and do something. Anything.

"I can't do this any more, so I'm ending it on my terms. I'm dying on Tuesday."

I'm dying right now. This isn't the *happily ever after* I wanted. But what did I expect? I'm here because my dad is dying. But I'm also here hoping he won't. Hoping he never does. Not after everything he's been through.

"I was going to do it earlier, but... I wanted to let you know first. I was just scared. Don't tell your mom. I don't think she would understand."

"Yeah, I won't say anything, Dad. I get it. It makes sense. I understand." I do. And I don't. There is no sense in this death. There's no sense in any of this.

"Oh, that's good. Thank you, Joshua."

I nod. Do you say *you're welcome* in a situation like this?

It's late. My dad makes another trip to his toilet chair, and I look away. The smell of acrid waste fills the air, and I turn to the sliding glass door and regret not opening it sooner.

We don't speak for the rest of the evening.

Anger

"I might have been wrong about my parents' relationship."

"Oh?"

"Maybe I should have been mad at my mom this whole time. Not my dad."

"Ok, wait. That doesn't make any sense. Your dad is the one who left."

"Is he? My mom moved to Korea and took me with her."

"But only because he said he was going to follow her there. He said he had some loose ends to tie up, remember?"

"I think my mom ran away from the situation. Why else would she move to Korea? She could have stayed."

"She said they agreed that being in Korea would give them a fresh start. Somewhere that they didn't have to try to explain their relationship."

"They shouldn't have had to. My mom took me and left, and my dad ended up homeless because of it. Now look at him. He's going to die."

"I don't think it's that simple, Josh. He smoked himself to death."

"I'm so mad. I'm mad at Angie, too."

"Why? What did she do? Oh, is she not—"

"No, she's not coming. She can't take the time off work or something stupid. Whatever, I'm glad she's not coming."

"What? You just said you were mad at her. Mad for not coming? Or mad she was going to show up in the first place?"

"I don't know! And do you know what? I don't even care right now."

"You seem upset. Did something happen?"

"What do you mean 'did something happen?' My dad is dying!"

"He's been dying the whole time you've been here, Josh. Why are you so upset right now?"

"What's with the interrogation? I'm not here giving you grief about everything you're saying."

"Do you want me to go?"

"What? No! I still want to talk to you. I need to talk to somebody about this."

"Ok. Just checking. I can be your sounding board. Just don't take it out on me, ok?"

Two

I wipe the sleep from my eyes and try to stretch. My body is cramped between the couch and the coffee table on the floor, and everything aches. I smell like an ashtray. The sliding glass door is slightly open to bring in some fresh air, but it doesn't make any difference. The emphysema that's killing my dad is trying to kill me, too.

Happy Father's Day.

My dad is watching the TV with the sound turned off and a cigarette in his mouth. He looks different to me now. Yesterday, my dad was waiting for a creeping death to claim him at some unknown time. Today, he's facing a beast that lives two days in the future. The phantoms know this date, too, and they're counting down.

"Oh, you're awake. Good morning, Joshua!"

I grunt and scoot myself to the sliding glass door to breathe. "Morning, Dad. Do you want a mocha?"

"Oh, that sounds nice. Yes, please."

"Ok. I'll head over there. Back in a bit."

I gather myself and rush outside the apartment building into breathable air, but taking in deep breaths doesn't help. No matter how much air I draw in, it doesn't feel like I'm breathing. Is this what drowning feels like?

I can't get last night's conversation out of my head. Hearing my dad describe the details of his condition brings me to the horrifying realization that the pain of my dad's life has never stopped. There's never been a happy ending. My dad's suffering has never ended. Between the emotional trauma of abuse and abandonment, the physical trauma of beatings and sexual assault, and now the torment of bodily deterioration, the darkness is claiming perpetual victory over my dad.

I let the rain fall on my face to hide my tears. What's the point of reconciliation if the story ends in death, anyway?

The Starbucks lounge is quieter this morning. The lobby is empty except for the four people in line. I sit at a booth and close my eyes.

It's nice that every Starbucks looks and sounds similar inside. It feels a bit like being transported to a safe and familiar place. It's not quite the feeling of being at home. More like a portal between the places we call home. The clinking metal, the smell of over-roasted coffee beans, and the hissing of the espresso machine behind the counter take me to that in-between place. Maybe I can rest here for a while.

There's something about the ambient noise that lets me tune

everything out so I can focus. It clears out my feelings so I can find emotional neutrality. From this blank space, I can conjure up feelings of strength or fear or weakness or hope.

I clear out the dread and darkness to find the quiet white noise of coffee shop meditation.

I don't know how long I've been drifting untethered in the other place when the woman behind the counter interrupts the peace. "Sir, can I help you?"

She can't. Nobody can.

I open my eyes, and the portal collapses. I'm thrust back into the Starbucks in Bend, Oregon, just outside my dad's assisted living apartment. This is the place of death.

"Sure." I saunter up to place my order. "One grande mocha. One grande americano, black. Both hot."

With a coffee in each hand, I shoulder open the Starbucks door and walk back to the apartment. Slowly. I try to recreate the slowness of time to force the clock to stop, but I can't. Every second that ticks forward shoves me closer to the cliffs of inevitability. There's a deadline on my dad's life. Deadline. Dead. Line. I sip my coffee and force myself up the stairs and back to the apartment.

"Happy Father's Day, Dad," I say while handing the mocha to him. He sits upright and takes the coffee.

"Oh, is that today?"

"Yup."

It's the last one. The last Father's Day. The last Sunday. I take another sip of my coffee and swallow the lump in my throat. It feels permanent now.

"So what's the latest in the news, Dad? What's going on in the world?"

"Have you paid much attention to the Bundy trial?" He points to the TV. A news anchorwoman is talking about the ongoing trial after the armed standoff between the Bundy family and Federal officers earlier this year.

"Not a whole lot. The Bundys occupied some land here in Oregon, right? I dunno. Something about cows."

"Yes, well... that's kind of a simplified view of it. There's a question about who has the right to be on Federal land and whether or not people should have to pay to use it."

"There was an armed standoff, right?"

"There was."

"Huh. Interesting." I shrug to hint at wanting to change the subject. It's an election year. I've had enough innocent political conversations turn into fierce debates, and I don't want to bring that kind of heat into this space.

"It's really important, Joshua."

"No, I know. I do think about these things."

He continues. "Most people on the left think the Feds are good, but they don't understand that Federal laws don't create the diversity and tolerance they want. If they did, that would be great. But instead, minorities are being targeted because the majority group is being strong-armed by the Federal government to change. So they get angry."

I can't help myself. I've debated these points in the past. "What about the civil rights movement? And women's suffrage? We have a whole Civil Rights Act and the 19th Amendment over this. That's the Federal government making important change, isn't it?"

"Joshua, those movements you're talking about paved the way *for* the Federal government. Not the other way around. The Civil Rights Act came about because people demanded it through the Civil Rights movement. The 19th Amendment was voted in because people demanded that women be able to vote. Is there a legitimate and powerful trans bathroom movement happening right now that would make any politician bet their career on it?"

My words are caught in my throat. "Well...ok. No, I suppose not."

"No, there isn't. The bathroom law was pushed through by Executive Order, and now trans people are less safe than they were before. They'll have to bug out and leave because of the backlash." My dad sighs and shakes his head. "It wasn't done right. Change needs to be phased in so the community can acclimate."

I stare at my dad while his eyes drift back to the TV. I have more I want to say to push back. I fight my instinct to debate.

"I don't disagree with the Bundys, Joshua," he says. The cigarette bounces in his lips with each syllable. "It's Federal land. Do you know what that means?"

"That it belongs to all of us?"

"That's exactly right. We're already paying for it with taxes."

"Yeah, that makes sense." This isn't the typical Left vs. Right conversation I'm accustomed to having about these issues. My dad's politics don't follow any convention I've ever encountered.

I try to relax and release the tension in my neck and shoulders. For years, any conversation related to politics would result in one-upmanship and an increase in volume to prove the other person wrong. Debating with my dad is the last thing I want to do. Maybe it's better to find peace. To sit in a space where I'm just curious. I'm learning about my dad's perspective on the world for the sole purpose of knowing him.

"Oh, shoot! Let me write all this down." I grab my notepad and pen and start writing. *Dad's politics.* I write what I can remember and just hope that I'll be able to fill in the gaps later. *Movements >> Federal Policy, not the other way around. Change must be phased in for acclimation. We paid our taxes.* Below that, I write *Lived experience vs. Political ideology. We don't need to debate everything.*

I look back up at him when I finish writing. "Well, Dad, with today being Father's Day, do you have any other important words of wisdom you want to pass down to me?" I say it with a tone of humor, but I really want to know him. I want to know if he's found any answers for his life. I assume every father has learned something they want their children to learn. Pitfalls to avoid. Struggles to prioritize.

My dad's eyes narrow. He leans forward like he wants to whisper something to me. His movement is so rapid and intentional that I forget he's dying. My dad's expression is serious. I nod in anticipation of his wisdom and ready my pen.

"If Trump wins," he starts. He peers out the open sliding glass door and then looks back at me. "If Trump wins, you're going to need to prepare."

I almost burst out laughing, but the gravitas in his voice stops me cold. He's not joking. I nod and try to appear attentive. I start writing.

"You need to brush up on your survival skills, do you understand? You'll want to know where your water supplies are. Get binoculars. Joshua, the right-wing may want to go to war. The landscape could change quickly; I want you to be prepared."

My pen flies to match speed with conspiracy.

"You need to establish good placement in the community. Find out who the influential people are. They're the ones people are following. From there, you can find people you can trust. You can band together and barter and protect each other."

I've tapped into a treasure trove of otherworldly strangeness. My dad's brow is furled while he speaks, and he keeps inching forward in his seat like he wants to stand. His words pour out with urgency. He is finally speaking like he is running out of time.

"… and then you need to figure out communication. Do you know anybody who owns a CB radio? Or HAM radio? And don't forget about securing your transportation."

"I think I'm probably ok, Dad," I say slowly to give myself time to catch up. My hand is cramping from writing. My mind is racing. This isn't the wisdom I was looking for, but it's giving me a glimpse of who my father is. Every warning, every word of caution and preparation have been tucked away in his mind, waiting for this moment. This is how my dad prepared himself against the perceived threats. This is how he wants to protect me.

"Listen, Joshua. You've got a lot of skills that will be useful. Metalworking, woodworking. It's important that people know what you can do so they know you're valuable. Valuable to the community."

He stops talking abruptly. I look up and see him staring at the TV again. I finish the last sentence he spoke and follow his gaze to the newscast. The latest presidential poll numbers show Donald Trump slipping considerably behind Hillary Clinton, and I nod and tap my notepad.

"This is all great information, but maybe I don't have to worry about doomsday, huh? It might not be an issue."

"It doesn't matter. You don't understand. He's going to win. You need to be prepared." His words are ominous, but I can't take him seriously. I write down *Be Prepared!* and close the notepad. My hand aches. My brain is full. I grab a couple Nutter Butter cookies and watch the TV, and rest.

It's not quite noon yet, and my dad remembers something. "Oh, Joshua, a minister or Chaplain is coming to visit later today. Around two, I think."

"Oh?"

"Yeah. Last rites or something. They do something like that here."

I nod, remembering again that my dad is dying. "Do you know how they handle the whole 'death with dignity' thing? Assisted suicide? I don't know what you call it, but I think a lot of Christians frown on that sort of thing."

"I didn't bother asking. I don't think what the minister thinks matters, though. Do you?"

This question stabs directly into my soul, and now, a new worry enters my mind. Does it matter? After the pure torment of my dad's entire life, will the people of my religion condemn him and promise another torment that lasts into eternity?

"No, I don't think it matters, Dad," I reply. I've thought about the morality of people who ended their own lives in the past. When I was in high school, a friend's cousin committed suicide. My friend asked if I thought her cousin was going to hell for it.

"I can't believe he's gone, Josh," Megan sobs. It's lunch break, and we have a few minutes before the bell rings for fourth period. Her hand is on my forearm, and she smells like vanilla.

I want to wrap my arms around her and hug her. I've had a crush on her for months, but I can't make a move now. Not after her cousin died. I feel terrible for her loss.

"I'm really sorry, Meg." I pat her hand, unsure what to say. "Were you guys close?"

"So close, Josh. You have no idea. We hung out all the time. He was like one of my best friends. I don't understand why he'd take his own life like that!" She wipes tears from her face.

"I wish there was something I could do," I reply, but I don't know what to say. I've never had anyone I know die before. I wish I knew Megan's cousin so I could grieve with her. At least that way, I could understand what she was going through.

She looks at me, and more tears stream down her face. "You're a Christian, right? Like, you go to church?"

"Sure," I say, almost reluctantly. It's not something I talk about much. I don't know what this has to do with the situation, but I don't want to appear unhelpful.

"Is my cousin...Is he in hell?"

My stomach drops, and I stutter. The details of church doctrine on suicide bubble to the surface of my mind, but the answers are academic. Cold and impersonal. I try to turn off the theology and just think about God as a person. Someone who cares for us, like the Bible says. "I... I... um... no," I finally say. As soon as I commit to my response, I picture

Megan's cousin grieving over his life, wanting more than anything to simply stop the pain he's in. He's in torment. "No, Megan. I don't believe he's in hell."

Her sobbing stops, and she stares into my eyes, pleading for reassurance. "Are you sure?"

"Listen, I know why people think all suicides lead to hell. It's because they think it's the ultimate insult to God. They think it's the same as telling God that He failed and that He's not strong enough to fix whatever problems they're having. But I don't think God is petty like that." The words come pouring out, and I have no idea where they are coming from. I was never taught any of this.

"If someone is legitimately broken and hurting, maybe from years of trauma or they're just messed up in the head, God isn't going to be angry at them because they made a bad choice. I don't even know if they *have* a choice. Nobody would choose suicide if they thought they had a better option. I don't think they believed they had a choice at all."

I continue with confidence.

"I don't believe God would take somebody's grief and pain and then decide to throw them into a lake of burning fire forever because He got mad at them for responding from a place of hurt. That doesn't make any sense at all."

Megan's grip on my forearm tightens and then releases. She nods and leans her head on my shoulder. The bell rings to signal the end of lunch. Five minutes to get to class.

"Thank you, Josh. I needed to hear that."

"Let me know if you want to talk later, ok?"

"Ok."

The memory fades, and I'm back in my dad's apartment, looking at the frail and broken totality of my dad's life. My answers to questions about heaven and hell are as certain as ever.

"I was actually going to go through with it last month, you know," my dad says. "I think I wasn't quite ready. I hadn't talked to you, yet. But also, I had a friend that wouldn't have had access to the meds in time so I gave my appointment to her."

"In time?"

"Yeah. She was dying, and she didn't want to suffer anymore. She suffered for so long. For some reason, she had a really difficult time making an appointment. They just kept pushing it further out. I told her she could have my appointment so she could die in peace last month. She was so thankful."

Thankful for death. My dad's words describe a tragic gratitude that fills the apartment. It was merciful for my dad to give up his appointment for her. It was a sacrifice to continue enduring his own suffering so someone else could finally rest.

My dad called this woman a friend. Does my dad have many friends? Is there solidarity to be found among people who are rejected by society and pushed to the margins? Do they hold one another in their grief? I don't know what the trans community is like. My dad said it was safe here in this part of Oregon, but that doesn't mean that my dad found community here. Nobody else has come to visit my dad to say goodbye.

Is this the case with most trans people, or does my dad's story just come with greater grief? I don't know, but it looks like I'm the only one standing for my dad. I suspect I'll be the one who reads the eulogy. I'll be the grieving person in the pews. I'll be the pallbearer. I'll be the one burying my father. My dad appears to have no one else.

I spend the next hour wrestling with the purpose of my dad's life. Why would God breathe existence into someone just to have them suffer? What was the point? How can people talk about a God of love and peace and then preach about a blessed hope in this life and in the life to come, only to be the very reason people like my dad have to suffer? My religion didn't accept my dad. It taught us to reject him. And now a Chaplain is coming to cast judgment as well.

It's two in the afternoon. There's a knock at the door that sounds like condemnation. I square my shoulders and prepare to defend my dad against the weight of oppressive religion and against a man who stands as the gatekeeper of the afterlife. I wonder if I'm bracing myself against God.

What is a Chaplain, anyway? Are they seeking some kind of confession or repentance to make vulnerable people "right with God?" My stomach turns at the thought of it.

"Come in, come in!" my dad cheerfully calls out. He drops his voice and whispers, "Minister" to me. He drags the blanket across his twig legs to hide their thinness and protruding veins. I'm already accustomed to my dad's withered state, but he seems embarrassed.

A man opens the door and says hello. He's a few inches shorter than I am and looks about my age. Tidy brown hair. Going a little bald on top. He's wearing a thin navy blue sweater over a cream-colored button-up shirt. Not at all like the Catholic priest I imagined. No real uniform. There's no ceremony about him at all. Clever.

"Hello, Anna," he says to my father. My hand reflexively raises, and I almost correct him. I hold my voice. I want to tell him that my dad's name is Sam to protect myself, but in doing so, I would expose my own inability to accept my dad's transgender identity. This tension between realities is splitting my soul. Is this Chaplain here because my dad wants to reconcile with God? He said Anna, so he knows that my dad is transgendered. Is he judging my dad?

Before my dad can respond to him, I dig my heels into the ground. I need proper footing. "You're Daniel," I say, pointing to his name tag. It says *Chaplain* beneath his name.

"Yes, hello," he says slowly. He follows my finger to the small plastic tag affixed to his pocket. "Yes, I'm Daniel. I'm the local Chaplain." He reaches out to shake my hand.

"I'm Josh. *Sam's* son." I reach out for a firm handshake to claim a position on the battlefield and study the response in his eyes. I hope for a look of surprise or an acknowledgment of the power I bring, but I'm immediately subdued by the warmth in his hand. I release my grip and lose the first battle of strength.

"Thank you, Josh. Nice to meet you." He withdraws his hand. "This must be a difficult time for you."

"Well, my dad's dying, so there's that." I feel the harshness in my voice. I try to relax my tone. "I guess you see a lot of that in your line of work."

"I've seen a fair share of death, yes." He nods and smiles. "But I try to keep it cheerful. Light. I tell jokes. Not very good ones." His eyes are kinder than I expected. Disarming.

There is a certain sadness about Daniel. The way he stands and leans slightly back on his heels. The way he holds his hands by his side when he talks. There's no fight in his posture. He looks vulnerable and defenseless. I wonder how many other dying people he saw today before knocking on my dad's door. How many per week? How much death has he seen?

"So what's that like, having to talk to people who know they're going to die soon? That sounds terrible."

"It's not always terrible." Daniel pauses briefly and then looks at the ceiling. "But sometimes… people aren't ready. So they fight it. It makes it a little harder." He blinks away the tears that are about to form.

"Oh, jeez. I didn't think about that." I picture the dying who would shrink away from the reality that Daniel represents.

"It's not just harder for them. It's hard for their family. And sometimes the family has a hard time letting go, too."

I nod and see these families in my head. They're all weeping and crying out for death to stay away, but they don't want their Chaplain to leave them alone, either. Daniel's world is the shores between life and death, and the waves crash where they crash. We stare at each other briefly, neither one of us speaking.

"Well, my dad's good and ready," I blurt out to break the painful silence. I give my dad a double thumbs-up, and he laughs in response. Daniel turns and smiles, but he doesn't say anything. He meets my dad's eyes, and then my dad ruffles his blankets on his legs. The uncomfortable awkwardness grows hot in the room.

I break the silence again. "So, do you know? I mean, about Tuesday?"

As the question leaves my mouth, I see it's not just one question. Contained in the asking is everything that I'm struggling to understand. I'm asking about the morality of assisted suicide and whether or not it insults God by demonstrating a damning lack of faith. I'm asking about God's view of transgender identities and if my dad's life represents a rejection of God's holy account of creation. I'm asking about prayers for healing and where the border between wishful thinking and divine hope in miracles exists. I'm asking about forgiveness and reconciliation between a son and his estranged father and what that requires. Does he know? And how does knowing affect his prayers for my dad? Does anyone know the mind of God? Or do we just suffer and wonder why?

"Yes, I know," he answers. But he's not answering the questions I want him to answer. "How are you dealing with it?"

"I'm dealing," I reply, guarded. I'm not ready to answer questions. "Hey, how did you get into the business of death, Daniel?"

His lips turn slightly downward, and he draws in a deep breath. He slowly exhales. I take that moment to grab my notepad. I write *Chaplain of Death* at the top.

"Well, I'm really in the business of comfort, Josh. Comfort for people who are scared or worried about... the future." His voice is calm, and his eyes are soft. I study his face for cracks in the persona. I can't tell if he is forcing this gentle composure or if he truly embraces it. Or if he lets it embrace him. I wonder how many people he's gently ushered across the threshold of the afterlife. I've never considered what the dying really want before the end.

I slowly scratch out the word *Death* and write *Comfort* beneath the scribbles. Perhaps I've been too quick to judge. But I need to know how he views God, and creation, and morality. How he reacts under pressure. I throw a grenade into the conversation.

"So what are your thoughts on free will versus predestination, Daniel?" I don't hold back. I press into him with perhaps the most divisive theological topic, fracturing entire church denominations and scattering believers in the aftermath. The consequences of either position create arguments that God is either weak or cruel, and I've argued from both sides of the debate. I'm not doing this for amusement. I need to know if the man before me can stand under theological scrutiny.

"I don't really know," he says. "I'm not too knowledgeable on the subject." He shrugs his shoulders.

I'm irritated at his lack of response and apparent lack of education. How was he credentialed? "But if you don't know whether or not God has predestined everything, how do you know if what you're doing even matters?" The words are bitter leaving my mouth. I'm completely dissatisfied with his answers.

He shrugs again. "I'm just here to deliver a message of hope to the dying, Josh. I've never really worried about the other details."

I furl my eyebrows and swallow down a realization. Perhaps I'm weak because I can't move forward without concrete answers. And perhaps it's me that's cruel. I'm the one demanding these concrete answers and creating division instead of finding peace and sharing it with people who need it.

That's all Daniel is doing. I want to apologize, but I'm ashamed.

"Well, you should probably talk to my dad, huh?" I want him to keep talking to me. The despair is still eating at me, and I don't have anyone to bring me comfort.

Daniel nods and then turns back to my dad. "Anna, is it ok if I sit on the couch next to you?"

"Of course," my dad says, smiling. He makes wide eyes at me again, but I don't know what he's trying to communicate.

Daniel is soft with his movements, his voice, and his whole way of being. He expresses a gentleness that can only be described as the fluttering of a dove. He sits beside my dad and holds his hands and offers to pray. My dad agrees, and the prayer is centered around Jesus as a savior who brings comfort, who is present, and who cares enough to stay by my dad's side through the infinite journey. My dad nods with his eyes closed. He says an *amen* in agreement at the end, but I don't know if my dad believes any of it.

Around the apartment, a collection of religious items grows in view. Crystals, crosses, a miniature Buddha. The skinny one from Thailand, not the jolly fat one from China. For all I know, my dad has looked for comfort in all the items.

In the apartment, amid the final prayers between my dad, a Chaplain, and the Creator of the universe, I wrestle with God. Was my dad's life broken for nothing? Can my dad be blamed for grasping at hope anywhere he can, whether in the mystical vibrations of purple amethyst crystals or in the calm eyes of the Theravada Buddha? I'm standing between my dad's broken body and the wrath of a jealous God. I'm still unsure.

Daniel stands and says goodbye to my dad. He approaches me and extends a hand. I clasp his in mine and pull him toward me into a hug.

"Will you be back again? Before Tuesday?"

"I won't. This is my last visit here."

"The last visit," I repeat back. My soul aches. I need more time. "The last prayer, huh?"

"No, I'll still pray for comfort. Tuesday, two o'clock. I have it on my calendar." He places a hand on my shoulder. "And you can pray for comfort, too."

None of my theology books have prepared me for grief. Daniel's words cut through the defensive fortress walls of religion and slice deep into my heart. Comfort is all I want.

We say goodbye, and I close the door behind the Chaplain and sit next to my dad.

"Are you ok?"

"Are you?" my dad asks back. His piercing green eyes are searching my soul.

Am I? I wanted to ask Daniel so many questions before he left. About assisted suicide and the morality of the trans community. I wanted to press him on those issues and share my anger at the religious establishment that he represented and that I grew up with. I thought that pinning down flaws in religious arguments and outflanking a minister on these heavy issues would make me feel better and more comfortable with heaven and hell.

But instead, comfort comes from something else. Not in the destruction or dismantling of religious dogma but in the simple prayer for comfort in the face of crushing uncertainty.

Bargaining

"Happy Father's Day."

"What? Oh, that's right. I thought about that this morning."

"Yeah? What in particular?"

"About how I've always just thought about myself for this holiday. I'm a dad. It's my day, right? I never really ever thought about my own dad on this holiday."

"Even as a little kid?"

"Oh, I guess I probably did. I don't really remember, though. I honestly don't remember a single Father's Day celebrating my dad."

"Too bad you don't have any siblings to repeat the stories and help jog that memory, huh?"

"Yeah, it's too bad about that. Now I wonder if my dad has any Father's Day moments from when I was little. I'll have to ask him."

"You might forget to ask him about it. It's ok."

"What?"

"*Nothing. Nevermind. So how was it? How was your Father's Day today?*"

"Well, I wish it was different."

"*It's not, though. It is what it is.*"

"Why does it have to happen like this? It's not like I wanted my dad out of the picture this whole time. I don't want him to die. I'm finally getting to know him."

"*Does it make you wish you could stop the clock? Maybe rewind it?*"

"Yes! That's exactly how I feel! I want a do-over. I want to do it all over."

"*Did the Chaplain rattle you a bit?*"

"No, it's not that. I thought that would be worse, but it went much more comfortably than I expected."

"*You thought he was going to say something hurtful, didn't you?*"

"I really did. I was ready to fight for my dad. Could you imagine somebody coming to your dad's deathbed and condemning them to hell because they couldn't get their head around being transgender or ending their own pain? I was so ready to hit that guy."

"*That's pretty violent, Josh. Aren't you a pacifist?*"

"I'm a 'thou shalt not kill' kind of pacifist. I don't have rules against punching people."

"*Ha! That's pretty good. I'm going to have to use that line.*"

"Go for it."

"There's got to be something I can do. Is there really no cure for emphysema? People have had full-blown lung transplants, haven't they?"

"I think so. But your dad isn't exactly young and healthy. And he's literally still smoking."

"So what if he quit? What if we tried to get him on a list or something?"

"Josh—"

"There's got to be a way to fix this. There isn't enough time to get all the stories."

"Josh, no."

One

The ache in my neck is a hot knife stabbing through the muscle and into the base of my skull. I'd say *it's killing me*, but that feels inappropriate. A crow is cawing outside, perched on the balcony rail. Perhaps Edgar Allen Poe's *Raven* is here to wake me from my painful sleep.

Nevermore. Nevermore.

I sit up and stretch my arms over my head. Yesterday was difficult, and I'm still wrestling with God.

"Oh, good. You're awake!" my dad says, breaking me free from the crow's spell. "There are a few things I want you to write down. Important stuff to take care of. I have some phone numbers for you." He speaks quickly and points to a folder at the end of the couch, just outside his reach. "You need to make some phone calls."

I'm barely awake, and my dad is far too energetic for someone who is dying tomorrow. It's eight in the morning, and I haven't had any coffee yet. I try to stretch through the sharp

pains in my body and wince with every new motion. The floor
has grown less comfortable with each passing night. After a
few awkward stretches, I grab the folder and flip through the
packets of paper inside. There's a brochure for a company on
top called BioGift. The caption under the title says *Your Final
Gift Could Last for Generations.*

"What's BioGift?" It looks like a brochure encouraging organ
donations, but I ask anyway.

"Oh, I'm donating my body to science, Joshua. A school
nearby wants to study me, and afterward, they pay for the
cremation. They make it so easy!"

He says all this without breaking eye contact. I think he's
probing for a reaction. Does he need me to be comfortable
contacting the company to handle the necessary paperwork?
Does he want to know if I'm alright with it? I've never
considered donating one's body to science or what might
happen if you do.

I've watched a few hospital-room dramas, and the scene I
imagine includes doctors and medical students standing around
a cadaver. The room has a very high ceiling and a large window
to an upper room. In that room are freshmen who aren't
allowed in the operating room, but they can watch the
procedure that's about to happen.

I can see all their faces. They're curious. Morbidly so. I
suppose that's appropriate. The body on the operating table
belongs to my dad, and these students are going to get an

education in transgender anatomy. There's going to be intense study and invasive exploration. But because I'm a little squeamish around blood and surgeries, the surgery room transforms into a kitchen scene. My dad is fully clothed, and his body is made of chocolate cake. The chief surgeon is cutting slices of my chocolate father and placing them on little plates for the students to study and eat. The freshmen upstairs stare longingly at the plates of cake.

Did my dad donate his body to save money? Or is he genuinely interested in advancing science and thinks donating his body is interesting and exciting?

I smile back at my dad and try to reassure him with a nod that I'm ok with this decision. Donating his body to science is the perfect ending for my dad.

My dad is a big Star Trek nerd. Donating his body to science seems connected to this. Perhaps instead of the hospital scene, my dad's body is in the *sick bay*, and members of the Starship Enterprise are scanning his body with their tricorders to learn more about this new alien species. Instead of using scalpels, they make precise laser incisions on his body, which instantly cauterize, leaving a perfect green alien scar. A red-shirted crew mate is eating cake he queued up in the replicator. (He'll be next on the sick bay bed, of course). I wish I could show this scene to my dad.

I flip through a few pages in the BioGift brochure and find their contact information.

"This is really cool, Dad. That's awesome that you're doing this. I'll call them. No problem."

"Good, good. You'll want to call them afterward. Call them on Wednesday."

Wednesday. The day *after*. What am I doing the day after? I try to imagine the next few days, but I can't. The image of my father dying looms in my vision, and I can't see anything beyond it. I'm spending all of my energy trying to remember the past. I'm struggling to stay afloat in the present. The reality of life after tomorrow is a complete fog.

"Yeah, Wednesday."

My dad is dying tomorrow. We're talking about what will happen with his body as though this is a casual conversation about anything ordinary. Furniture. Traffic. Donating his body to science. I'm stuck in this surreal world of casual death and Nutter Butters.

A loud knocking at the door breaks me free from the strangeness. Before my dad can answer, the door swings open, and a man in a raggedy black leather coat and dirty jeans blunders in. A matching black Labrador retriever pushes past his legs and joins him in the cacophony of motion and noise. The dog's tail knocks my to-do folder off the coffee table, and when the dog spins around to examine the pile, the leash gets wrapped around its legs.

I take a deep breath. It's my dad's old friend, Curtis.

"Curtis, you made it!" My dad raises his arms, and Curtis

shuffles his towering frame over to the couch to hug him. He drops the leash on the way, causing it to tumble and zip between the couch and coffee table. The flailing leash startles the dog, who leaps back into me, nearly knocking me to the floor.

"Oh, don't mind Jojo!" Curtis calls out while still hugging my dad.

I've met Curtis before. Just once, about seven years ago. Curtis and my dad visited us when we lived in the Lacey house. That's when my dad brought the Barbie doll house for the girls. Curtis came with him.

At the time, my dad said Curtis was his *friend*. I wondered if he was more than this, but I never asked. I didn't like him. He made me uncomfortable, and I assumed he was somehow preying on my dad's vulnerability. There was a look in his eyes that made me uneasy. Unsettled. I'm not sure how to feel about him now. He takes up so much air in this room.

But Curtis is clearly still around. He brings his dog. Maybe he's a part of my dad's life. My assumptions about Curtis taking advantage of my dad might have been wrong. I'll admit, he has a different look in his eyes. Maybe Curtis is my dad's only friend in the world. If this clumsy, disheveled heap of a man brought joy to my dad in any small way over the years, perhaps I should be thankful.

He turns back to me and opens his arms for a hug. I nod, and before I can extend my arms, he grabs me and pulls me in.

He smells like body odor and a different brand of cigarettes than the ones my dad smokes.

After releasing me from his embrace, Curtis and my dad catch up like old friends who haven't seen each other in a while. I learn a few things about Curtis' life. He lives alone with Jojo. He picks up odd repairman jobs here and there without a license, and he pirates newly released movies. He's offered to share a few with my dad, but my dad politely declines and reminds him that there isn't enough time to watch movies.

The room grows bright. Everything in the room glows with iridescence, and their conversation pushes back shadows and darkness and sadness. They're two friends talking about life, and the room is vibrant with it. I'm only here because of death.

While they talk, I open the sliding glass door and stand on the balcony. It's gray outside again, and there's a cool breeze. The crow is gone. I shut the door behind me to give Curtis and my dad space.

I'm glad Curtis is here, for my dad's sake. I'm glad that my dad had a friend in this world to keep him company and who finally came to visit. But with less than a day remaining, I struggle to weigh the value of my time against Curtis'. I need this time. Curtis had my dad to himself for years.

I can feel the selfishness. I know it's only right that Curtis gets this time. He put in the effort and walked with my dad for years. He was a companion and friend. I never even bothered to reach out.

The sliding glass door opens, and Curtis joins me on the balcony and closes the door behind him. He lights a fresh cigarette and leans over the railing next to me.

"I don't... I don't really agree with this death stuff," Curtis stammers. His eyes are freshly red, and his voice is low, gravelly. He stands closer to me on the balcony and whispers. "I'd stop it if I could. I...I mean, wouldn't you? Is there anything you can do?" Puffs of smoke escape his mouth as he talks.

I stare at the irony in front of me. Curtis is smoking cigarettes while grieving the condition of my dad, who is dying from smoking cigarettes. I'm annoyed. I try to look past the smoke so I can study his face. There's so much grief in his eyes. Grief and desperation. He's pleading with me to stop my dad from ending his life. He thinks I have the power to change my dad's mind.

Curtis has been around for as long as I've been gone. They traveled together. They went camping together. They moved from town to town together as friends. Curtis didn't have to keep my dad company, but he did. They were friends. If this was my dad's only friend, maybe my dad is Curtis' only friend. This loss might be greater for Curtis than it will be for me.

Would I stop my dad's decision if I could? Could I try to convince him to push through and hope for some miraculous healing in his lungs that could extend his life?

"He's suffering, Curtis," I finally say. "I don't think he wants to suffer anymore. I don't want him to suffer anymore, either."

"I know, I know. You're right. I know." His greasy hair flops from side to side as he shakes his head. He takes a long puff on his cigarette and blows another gray cloud into the sky. He opens the sliding glass door and steps back inside.

"Anna, I think we're gonna go. I'll be back tomorrow." He pats Jojo on the head, and the dog presses into his leg.

"You'll be here? Will you really? You said you weren't sure earlier."

"Yeah, I'll be here." He turns around and gently tugs on Jojo's leash. "Come on, boy. Let's get going. See you tomorrow, Josh."

I watch my dad's face to try to see what he's feeling. There is a sadness that I'm trying to understand. Does he want Curtis to stay? If I wasn't here, would my dad be able to spend his last days with his friend instead of me? Would he prefer that? I feel a little self-conscious now about my presence here. Maybe I'm the one intruding. I'm the one who doesn't belong here.

"I love you, Curtis. I'll see you tomorrow."

"Tomorrow," he mutters under his breath. "Love you too." Curtis and Jojo head out the door, and the apartment grows quiet again.

My dad smiles at me, and the room's glow returns to normal. My normal. My dad's green eyes light a path through the forest, guiding me back to our relationship. Any insecurity I have about Curtis and who my dad wants to spend time with is washed away by a clear stream that gently flows between the trees. The room becomes the forest where I can rest. I can lie down. My dad's eyes tell me that he wants me here. He's always wanted me here. Home.

How does anyone live without this sense of home? How did I live for so long without it? And how am I going to survive when the forest burns tomorrow?

I blink away the trees and study my dad's face. "Are you ok, dad?"

"Me? I'm fine. I just hope Curtis shows up tomorrow. He's having a tough time with this."

"Well, it's a hard thing to face, Dad. I'm having a tough time with it, too."

"Curtis told me before that he didn't want to come. He wasn't going to. I think he's scared. I really wasn't sure he was going to make it."

"Yeah. Makes sense. It's hard."

"I hope he can make it, for his sake."

I suddenly understand what my dad is saying. He knows that the emotional weight of death isn't really on his shoulders. It's going to be carried by the rest of us that he leaves behind. The dying are free from that burden. My dad isn't trying to fight against death as it drags him into the earth. He's choosing to go on a journey. My dad told the Chaplain that he was at peace, and looking into his eyes, I believe him. Maybe the phantoms really have no power here.

If Curtis doesn't come to say goodbye, he will only hurt himself. It will haunt him every time he thinks of my dad. For the sake of their friendship and for his own peace, I hope he can make it tomorrow, too.

"Dad, I'm going to break away for a bit. I haven't eaten. I think I'm getting a little jittery. I'm going to grab something from Safeway, ok?"

"Ok, get what you need. I'll see you when you get back."

"Do you want anything? Do you want more Bugles?"

"I really can't keep them down, Joshua. But I'll take a mocha, though," he says with a grin.

"No problem. Back in a bit." I take two steps towards the door and stop. "Actually, Dad, I haven't seen Kendra and the girls in a while. Is it ok with you if I have a late lunch with them? And then maybe have them come up and say hi real quick?"

I don't really mean "hi." I mean "goodbye." The last goodbye.

He nods, and I see that he knows exactly what I mean. "Of course, Joshua."

I leave the apartment and text Kendra on the way down the stairs. She agrees to join me for lunch, and within ten minutes, my family shows up at the apartment to pick me up.

"Josh, there isn't enough room in the car for all of us," Kendra says from the passenger seat. "There's only room for five."

I inspect the sky for rain. It's overcast.

"It's fine. The place I want to eat is just up the street. I can walk and meet you guys there."

"Where?"

"There's a pizza and sandwich shop on the right. It's the same side of the road as the apartment."

"Ok, we'll meet you over there."

I briskly walk the short distance to the restaurant and watch Kendra gather the girls as they scramble out of the back seat of the rented car. She looks frustrated. My mom looks exhausted. The jet lag from Korea is always rough on her, and it can take days for her to adjust. Kendra has been single-parenting our three daughters out of an RV for a few days now, and I feel bad for her.

We clamor into the restaurant, but I'm the only one who orders food. Everyone else has already eaten. I can hear Kendra trying to shush the girls at one of the tables behind me, but the noise only grows louder. I apologize to the young woman who is taking my order, and then I rejoin my family.

The girls haven't stopped talking about their shopping trip from earlier today.

"How are you managing, Kenge?" I ask. She's resting her cheek on her hand. "Long shopping trip?"

"I don't know how single moms do it," she says through gritted teeth. "I know they do. I know it can be done, but it's just exhausting, even with your mom's help. It's like the girls don't get tired anymore!"

My mom nods and shuts her eyes briefly. Kendra and I exchange glances that tell me she wishes she had more help.

"I'm not tired!" Charlie chimes in helpfully. She smiles like she's had too much sugar and immediately returns to talking with her sisters.

"I'm so sorry, Kendra. I didn't think about how this trip would affect you."

I've been drawing closer to my dad each day. I'm trying to tie up decades' worth of loose ends while my wife's days unravel. I feel terrible. I haven't given her any thought at all. Her eyes beg for help, and I haven't been around to provide it. How do I navigate being a good husband to my wife and father to my daughters while also trying to be an honorable son? Can I do both?

I want to comfort her. I want to tell her that she doesn't have to endure much longer and that this difficulty is almost over. Just one more night. Tomorrow, I'll join my wife in the RV. The cost of returning to my family is saying goodbye to my dad.

Just a little bit longer, Kendra.

"Hey, when we're done here, do you guys want to swing by the apartment and say hi to my dad?"

"Is he doing ok?" Kendra asks, and then she leans in. "Is he getting worse?"

"Off and on. His difficulty breathing comes and goes," I say. It's not really a lie. "But he's been feeling pretty good today, so I thought it'd be nice to get a quick moment in. Who knows if it'll be the last opportunity?"

Kendra shoots me a questioning look, and I see a twitch between her eyebrows. I pretend like I don't notice.

"Girls, do you want to come back to the apartment and say hi to Papa Sam?"

"Yeah, as long as Mom can breathe ok," Olivia answers. She looks at Kendra with a dramatic expression of concern. Kendra laughs.

"I'll be able to visit Papa Sam for a little bit. Don't you worry, Olivia," Kendra says through a smile.

"It'll be quick, Olivia. It won't be a whole introduction again. Just coming up to say hi and to hope Papa Sam doesn't feel too sick."

"Ok, we can do that," she concludes with a single nod. She tells her sisters the plan and gets their approval as well.

"Girls, do you want to know what Papa Sam and I are talking about?"

"Yeah!" they all reply. Even Libby, who has been quiet.

"Well, my dad has this really neat book about how to survive..." I raise my hands slowly into the air and open my eyes wide. I look at them individually and then dart my fingers towards their faces. "An alien invasion!"

They burst out laughing. They don't believe me, so I assure

them that the book is real. I promise to show it to them.

"Oh, and my dad has this really cool leopard gecko named Deuce."

"Deuce? That's a funny name," Libby says. Her nose is wrinkled when she repeats the name.

"Yeah, super funny. Did you know that some people say *deuce* as another way to say... poop?"

The girls laugh again. Even my mom laughs. Kendra just smiles at me and shakes her head.

"Oh, that reminds me, Kendra. Do you remember when my dad brought that Barbie house to us? Do you remember his friend, Curtis?"

"Yeah, kind of. He didn't really talk that much."

My mom's face scrunches up in disgust. "That Curtis, he was such a strange man. I didn't like him."

"Well, I didn't like him at the time, either. But he's still around. He stopped by today while I was there."

"Oh, so they're still friends," Kendra says. The way her voice dips at the end of her statement tells me what she's thinking. She's always wondered if there was a physical relationship between my dad and Curtis. More than friends. I never gave it any thought. It's easier not to. I'm not going to ask.

I finish my sandwich and we spend a few minutes trying to get the girls focused enough to follow us to the car instead of running around the tables of the empty lobby.

"Who gave them all the sugar?"

Kendra elbows me in the ribs and whispers, "Your mom, of course. Donuts."

"Ah. She does like donuts."

"Well, she told each girl to pick their own instead of having them split a couple. How am I supposed to get all of their energy out? The RV isn't big enough!"

I grab Kendra and hug her. We hold each other while the girls swirl around us like dust devils. My mom chases them around the lobby and finally ushers them outside and to the car. I don't let go of Kendra. We stand in the lobby together and I try to ignore the stares of the employees.

Kendra eventually pulls away from me and wrinkles her nose. "You smell so bad, Josh."

"Sorry. I'd shower, but I'm still sleeping on my dad's floor. I don't think I'm ever going to smell good again," I tell her. She plugs her nose and sticks her tongue out at me.

We leave the restaurant together, our fingers intertwined, and I walk her to the car door. The girls are already buckled and waiting, and my mom is in the driver's seat. There's a light drizzle that threatens to become rain, so I kiss Kendra and jog back to the apartment. I wait for them to park.

When I step inside, the black hole of the elevator doors promises to swallow me, my family, and the whole world. I'm leading them to the final moments of my dad's life, and they have no idea. They'll say goodbye. No matter what happens, they won't linger long enough. They won't savor the moment and hold on, wishing the day would last. Wishing tomorrow wouldn't come.

I don't even try to resist being pulled into the darkness. But this is my darkness, not theirs. My family is here to say hello. They have no idea that they're saying goodbye. I lead the way into the abyss. My abyss.

When the doors open again, I try to count our steps on the worn carpet to my dad's apartment. The girls rush ahead, and I lose them around the corner. Kendra and my mom stay close to me and match my slow pace. These are the last steps they'll take to see my dad while he is still alive.

The hallway of dread stretches into the distance, where my girls are huddled together in front of my dad's door. Every one of my steps brings them closer to the end. I watch each of my feet move forward, inching closer to the gentle lie I have to tell them. Is there a way for me to have them stay longer? Is there anything to be gained?

I knock on the door to give my dad time to cover his legs. He invites us in, and my family waits behind me, still cautious. Hesitant. Whether it's the smoke or the simple discomfort of being in the presence of the dying, they stand outside the door for a brief moment before following me in.

"I finished lunch and thought I'd bring everybody by to say hi since you're feeling better today," I say. I make knowing eye contact with my dad, and we conspire in our mixed truth.

"Oh, hi, everyone," my dad replies while waving them in. He extends his hands to my daughters, who allow him to embrace them. He looks at each of them and tells them how much he values them. How beautiful they are, and how lucky they are to have a caring mom and dad. His green eyes cast the room into the edge of the forest, where a slow river touches the shore.

This is his goodbye to my family. A goodbye without grief. My dad is navigating the unknown waters of almost-death. The waters are calm right now - no tears, no sadness. No dangerous rapids or threats of injury. No need to help my wife, my mom, and my daughters cope. My dad is free to say goodbye in peace. He doesn't need to comfort the living.

There's a peace here I didn't expect. This secret I'm keeping with my dad is saving my family from mourning too early. They already know he's dying, so their time with him should be spent finding moments of joy in his presence. This leaves space for my dad to save the energy he needs to embark on his final journey.

Kendra and my mom draw close to my dad. They each hold his hands for a moment before nodding and turning back. The time spent is enough. This somber moment of this family ceremony is sufficient.

I walk my family back down to the car and hug them. I tell them that I'll see them tomorrow. I watch them drive away in the rain, and once they leave the parking lot, I finally let out a sigh of relief.

While I walk the stairs back up to my dad's apartment, I mull over the things I want to talk about with him. I want to ask him about this experience with this strange hello and goodbye and see if he views it like I do. But before I can say anything, my dad interrupts my thoughts when I enter the apartment.

"Joshua, I have some money. I don't need it, and I want to give it to you."

"Ooh! An inheritance!" I say with cartoonish enthusiasm. My dad can't have much money. Between the cost of the apartment and the assisted living care, his Social Security checks can't go very far.

"Well, I guess so. It's just a couple thousand dollars. I know it's not much, but I want to make sure you get it."

A couple of thousand dollars is probably months and months of savings for my dad. Did he set aside this money every month, knowing this day would come? Or did he not know what to spend the money on when he was healthy enough to enjoy it?

"Alright, Dad. Do you have an ATM card? I can run to the bank and pull it out. That should be easy enough."

"No," he replies flatly.

"No? Why not?"

"I don't trust them."

My ears ring, and red threads vibrate across the room. Of course, he doesn't trust them. I shift my view and see the threads spread out into a fully formed web. I try to make sense of them. There's a shimmering red line starting at the word "convenience" on one end of the room and it's connected to my wallet and my phone. Another thread starts at "security and privacy," and the threads from there touch everything else in the room. Maybe convenience isn't worth the loss of control. Maybe targeted advertising and data leaks reveal the sinister underpinnings of the entire Internet. The threads glow brighter. I shake my head to make them disappear so I don't make too many connections myself.

"Well, that complicates things a little. Can you come to the bank with me?"

There's a knock on the door. Steve calls from the other side.

"It's me, Anna," he says.

"Come in," I reply, answering for my dad.

Steve trudges in, and I wonder if I can catch a glimpse of death on him. Is there a common look among those who are dying? I watch him clear the few dishes I've used, looking for any hint of terminal illness. I don't notice anything different about him. When he grabs the crickets for the leopard gecko, my dad breaks the silence.

"Steve, I think I want you to take Deuce. You've been caring for him since I got him, and I'd like you to have him."

"No, Anna. I won't do that."

"Oh! Well, why not?" My dad looks at me, and I see he's genuinely surprised.

Steve stands still and sets the bag of crickets down. He doesn't look up. "My cancer isn't good. I don't know how long I'll be able to take care of myself, much less this gecko."

I watch my dad's shoulders slump.

"I'm... sorry, Steve. I'm really sorry. Is there anything I can do?"

It's a strange scene. My father will die tomorrow. He is trying to comfort a man who may succumb to cancer in the future. How can he possibly help?

"Um, I can take care of the gecko, Dad. I'm sure Kendra won't mind."

"Oh, good. I was going to ask you next, anyway. You can ask Steve how he feeds Deuce. He says it's pretty easy."

I don't ask him. Steve doesn't seem to be in the mood to talk, and when I stand up and walk to the counter to see what he's doing, he just points at the tub of calcium powder and tells me to make sure I dip the crickets into it before giving it to Deuce.

After Steve finishes cleaning the counters, he says goodbye and leaves. The bag of crickets sits on the counter for me.

"He's not taking it very well," my dad says after the door closes.

"His cancer?"

"No, me. I told Steve about tomorrow, and he got pretty mad about it. He hasn't really talked to me much since then."

"Oh. Has he been your caretaker for very long?"

"For a couple of years. I was certain he wanted to take Deuce to keep him as a companion. He really liked that gecko."

I decide to let my dad believe that. "His cancer must be pretty serious then, huh?" There's no need to change my dad's story.

"I don't really know. He hasn't talked about it at all. Just that it's terminal."

What do the dying talk about? What stories do the dying share? I always imagined that the dying expressed their regrets towards the end. About all the things they wished they could have accomplished but didn't have time to do. Or didn't prioritize.

My dad hasn't mentioned any regrets.

Depression

"I'm running out of time. What's the point of all this? I'm trying so hard to write down as much as I can, but there's no way to capture it all. There's just no time."

"This sounds a bit like the library thing."

"Library thing?"

"You know, the whole thing about you going into a library and having it stress you out because you know you can't read all the books."

"Oh. I mean, yeah. It's just like that. The deeper I go into the library, the more books I see that just add to what I'll never know. Every minute I spend with my dad, the more I realize how much about him I just won't have time to learn."

"It's like Wheeler's quote. As our island of knowledge grows, so too does the shore of our ignorance."

"Well that's depressing. You're supposed to be helping me."

"Am I?"

"What the heck? Of course, you're supposed to help me. You know me. You're the only one who knows how I think."

"So you want me to agree with you?"

"No, of course not. That wouldn't help. But this isn't helping either."

"There's absolutely nothing I can do. You already know this."

"What's the point, then? My dad is dying tomorrow. Tomorrow! I don't want tomorrow to come."

"But don't you want his suffering to end?"

"Of course. But that means that my suffering starts, doesn't it?"

"Do you think that's a fair trade? Your suffering for his?"

"No, of course not. That's not the same thing. Ugh. I just hate this. I hate this so much."

Zero

It's 4:28 in the morning. My vision is blurry from the sleep in my eyes. I try to lie perfectly still to listen to whatever woke me up but I don't hear anything.

It's too early to be awake. I lift my head to look outside, but there's no light coming in through the sliding glass door. Maybe nobody is awake in this sleepy town of Bend, Oregon. Just darkness that seeps into everything, like one of the final plagues of Egypt before God's avenging angel kills the firstborn sons of the land. In the story, the tenth plague could kill a firstborn father and his firstborn son. I wonder if God will kill us both on this final day.

I lay my head back down and shut my eyes to shake off the gloom. It's definitely too early to be awake. How many hours are left? I'm too sleepy to do the math. I shut my eyes and hope time stands still.

I snap out of sleep and tear my sleeping bag open. What time is it? The clock says nine in the morning. I groan and throw my head back onto my pillow. I've lost four and a half hours. I inhale sharply and wince at the stabbing pain in my chest. Is this just more body aches from sleeping on the ground? Is this heartache?

I only have four hours left. My heart is pounding.

Through stiffness brought on by discomfort and grief, I force myself to sit up and look around the room. My dad is watching TV. He doesn't look any different today than he did yesterday. I wish he did. I wish my dad looked worse than he does right now. He doesn't look like someone who has scheduled their death for two in the afternoon on a Tuesday in June. I wonder how long he would live if he didn't decide to die today.

The folder with the to-do list is on the table next to the alien survival book.

"I'm going to the bank now, Dad. Hopefully, I can get it sorted. I'll call you if there's anything I need from you."

"Ok, Josh. I'll be here," he says with an odd amount of cheer in his voice.

I can't shake the image I had when I first heard that my dad was dying. I pictured him laid up in a hospital bed, barely coherent, sleeping for most of the day with a morphine drip to keep the pain at bay. He's just laying there, basically gone before he dies, and the only evidence that he's alive is a heart monitor that's beeping away.

This situation with my dad is so different than what I

imagined. When my dad says, "I'll be here," it feels like something an ordinary dad says to his ordinary son on an ordinary Wednesday morning.

Your father is going to die!

Today is the last day he'll say it. When he passes, the phantoms will grow silent, too.

There's a few more Nutter Butter cookies on the counter. My dad isn't supposed to eat anything for 24 hours, so I grab the remaining cookies before heading out the door.

I leave my dad's apartment and force myself into the elevator. The elevator doors close, and I wish I was still daydreaming. I wish that when the doors opened, the California heat would pour in, and I'd be back in Dinuba. Maybe I'm back in my office in the middle of another life insurance presentation, and I'm about to fall back out of my dream of the Olympic National forest.

The elevator *dings*. The doors open, and I'm not in California. I'm still in the assisted living apartment in Bend, Oregon, and I'm within the last few hours of my dad's life. I die a little with every broken hope.

Outside, the wind is driving the rain into my face. A chill in the air bites into my flesh so I draw my jacket tightly around me. I'm unsuccessful at avoiding puddles as I dodge cars in the Safeway parking lot. I curse my wet socks and the rain and then regret speaking ill of my lifelong friend. I'm glad it's raining. I'd hate for my dad to die on a beautiful summer afternoon.

Just inside Safeway, the US Bank is open. There's no line at the unusually tall counter. The only bank teller is a young woman who yawns and looks blankly forward into the heart of the grocery store. I follow her gaze down the aisle of chips and soda, but she notices me and calls me to the window.

The height of the counter forces me to look up at her, and I wonder if this is how short people always feel. I'm distracted by the view into her nostrils. I try to look away and focus on something else. I notice that her name tag is covered by her long black hair.

"Hi, ma'am. I have a problem, and I hope you can help. It's pretty complicated."

"Ok," she responds slowly. She stares down at my black hoodie and ripped jeans with a frown. Between my appearance and what I'll ask next, it will look like I'm trying to commit fraud.

"So… my dad," I begin. I consider the complication of the pronouns, but I decide not to explain. But then again, if I can get the account pulled up, I'll have to use my dad's other name. His legal name. "My dad lives at the assisted living apartments across the street, and he wants to close his account. He's dying, and I guess I'm inheriting the funds." I shrug. What must this teller think of my nonchalant explanation of such a tragic event? How do I make this sound less like a scam?

"Ok, sir. Your father will need to come in here and provide

identification if he wants to empty his account. Then he can do whatever he wants to do with it." Her lips pull tightly as she smiles. She leans back and places her hands on the counter. She definitely doesn't believe me.

"Unfortunately, my dad is bedridden." I shrug again. Why do I keep shrugging? "If he can't make it into the bank, what would he need to do to make this happen?"

She snaps a business card from the counter and thrusts it at me. "Here. There's an 800 number he can call. They might be able to provide him with some additional solutions, but without him physically here in the branch, there's nothing I can do to withdraw funds or close the account. I'm afraid I can't help you."

I look at the phone number and back up at her. I want to tell her that I'm not trying to scam anyone, and I'm not committing elder abuse. I'm here at my father's bidding to fulfill his last wishes. It won't help, and I don't have time.

I rush back to the apartment to tell my dad the situation. I don't even try to avoid the puddles on the way back.

Even if the teller believed me, she'd need to verify my dad's identification. Someone would need to sign documents, I'm sure of it. I slip off my wet shoes and socks and try to conjure solutions for my dad's money, but none come to mind.

"I can't withdraw money from the bank without you being there. Not without a card or something," I relay to my dad. "To the bank, I'm nobody."

"Did they give any options?"

"Not without you being there. It doesn't matter that you're literally at Death's door. They gave me a number to call, though."

I flip the business card over a few times and call the number. After working through several voice prompts, I finally speak to a real person.

"This is Katrina with US Bank. How may I help you?"

I put the phone on speaker so my dad can hear. "Hi, my name is Josh. I'm calling for a really important request. My dad is dying, and we're trying to see how we can withdraw money from his account." I make eye contact with my dad as I'm saying it, and he nods. There's nothing I can do to avoid sounding like I'm trying to steal my dad's money.

"I'm near a US Bank branch in a Safeway in town, so I can get over there, but I don't have a way to get my dad there. He's not healthy enough to go. I don't really know what the next step is. Can you put in a note on his account or something with my dad's verbal authorization so I can go to the bank and close the account on his behalf?"

"No, I'm sorry. Your father would have to go to the bank in person and provide his identification. Now, if he has an ATM card—"

"No, he doesn't have one," I interrupt. I wish *conspiracy theorist* was a legitimate excuse that would allow me to bypass the security. "Is there anything else we can do? My dad is literally dying, and we need to get this done today."

"No, unfortunately, there's no way for us to be able to close the account and withdraw the funds."

"There's got to be something. This hasn't happened before? What happens, then? I have to wait for probate to claim my dad's estate of a few thousand bucks? This is kind of ridiculous, ma'am."

"Sir, not without him there or a Power of Attorney. There's nothing I can do."

I roll my eyes and look at my dad. He shrugs.

"Ok. I'll just have to try something else. Thanks anyway."

"Thank you for calling—"

I hang up the phone and close my eyes. I can't think of any easy solutions.

"Dad, you don't happen to have a check, do you?"

"I don't know if I do." He points to one of the smaller cardboard boxes under a stack of papers closest to the TV. "Maybe look in there?"

Why would my dad have a check? I open the box and rifle through the contents. There are official-looking documents and doodles on small scratch sheets of paper. A small handmade leather pouch. I open it to see if there's anything inside, but it's empty. Under the pouch are a few bottle caps. I keep pulling junk out of the cardboard box, and then I freeze. At the bottom of this box of random junk, there's a US Bank check with my dad's name on it. *Anna Brennan.*

"What on earth?! Why do you have this in there?" I hold the minor miracle up in my hand.

My dad shrugs. "I thought it might be in there."

"How is this possible? And it's just this one check?" I dig into the box again and push more junk around the bottom. "Not even a checkbook?"

"Will that work?" he asks.

It feels like I witnessed magic. "Yes, oh my gosh, yes! This should work. If your money is in your savings account, we just need to move it to your checking account. I think we can do *that* over the phone."

I press redial on my phone and navigate the voice prompts again.

"Hi - I just called a little bit ago. I'm not sure who I spoke with or if they took down any important notes, but I have a challenging situation." I describe it again for the third time, and it feels like a script I've had to memorize. I add the new line. "I need to see if we can move money from the savings account to the checking account."

"Yes, let me pull up the account. So you want to move how much from savings to checking?"

"All of it. It should be about three thousand."

"Yes, ok. Is the account owner there with you? I know they gave you the authorizing information, but we need verbal confirmation from them on this recorded line.

My dad nods, and I bring the phone closer to him.

"Ok - let me get him on the phone. He's having a hard time breathing, so it might be hard for him to say very much. I've got him close to the phone now. Go ahead."

"Ok, Anna - are you able to hear me?"

"Yes," my dad says, weakly.

"Ms. Brennan, do you authorize this transfer of $3,002.15 from your savings account to your checking account?"

"Yes, thank you."

"I'm sorry. Can you repeat that?"

I bring the phone closer to my dad's face. "Yes, thank you!"

"Ok, Ms. Brennan, I went ahead and moved the funds in the amount of $3,002.15 from your savings to your checking account. Is there anything else I can help you with?"

I pull the phone back to me. "Yeah, it's me, Josh, again. I plan to write a check from the account for the whole amount. That'll empty it. Do I need to wait before doing that, or can I write the check immediately?"

"The funds are in there now, so you can do it immediately if you wish."

"Ok - thank you so much. This should do it."

"You're welcome, and thank you for being a customer of US Bank."

Not for long, I think to myself as I hang up the phone.

"Ok, Dad. I think this will work!" I grab the check and fill it out. "Do you want me to sign it for you?"

He nods. I flip the check over and pen the name *Anna*

Brennan on the endorsement line, and the mixture of excitement over finding this check and the twisted pain of writing my dad's name makes me feel suddenly lightheaded. I've never written that name before.

I grab my phone and open my bank app to deposit the check without looking at my dad. My mouth feels dry. I wonder if my dad wished I referred to him by his new name. Or if he wished I used the feminine pronoun.

The deposit works. My bank immediately posts the deposit, and I exhale.

"It worked, Dad."

"Good, good, I'm so glad about that. I don't know what would happen to the money if you couldn't get it. I don't want the bank to keep it, that's for sure."

I grab a fresh set of socks and my notepad from my backpack and sit on the floor in front of my dad's couch. Closer to him, this time.

The clock reads ten o'clock. I have three hours left. I flip past a few pages I've filled and set the tip of my pen at the top of a new blank page.

"Dad, I want to write down as much as I can about you. Your life. I want to know more of your stories."

He looks at me with a slow smile. The crow's feet beside his sunken eyes are deep ravines filled with stories of tragedy. The greatest of horrors. I worry that asking him to tell me about his past will dredge up pain, but I need to know these stories.

"Well, I had a good life, I think."

I write those words while my dad speaks them, but my eyes widen as my pen captures this statement. For me, the entirety of my dad's story has been the opposite of *a good life*. It's full of heartbreak, betrayal, tragedy. It's the life we try to avoid. It's the life we warn our kids to avoid. What could my dad mean by this?

"A good life, huh?"

"I'd say so. I came up during the fifties. Back then, the nation was very immature as far as civil rights go. It was the McCarthy era."

"The big bad communism, huh?" I recall learning about *McCarthyism* in college.

"Right, right. We were still recovering from World War Two, and now people were very nervous about the threat of communism with the Korean War going on. Patriotism was a really big deal back then."

"It's still a big deal now. Especially now with this election cycle. Have Republicans always claimed that Democrats were communists?"

"Well, yeah, but this was back when it was an actual threat. It's all boogieman now."

I sketch a hairy monster next to *Communist Boogieman*. It's just a ball of stringy hair with military boots and a hammer-and-sickle logo.

"It was a very conservative time. Everybody back then was

reading or talking about Dr. Ben Spock and the Bible. They were two of the greatest influences on the culture back then."

I don't know who Dr. Ben Spock is, so I make sure to spell it out so I don't confuse it later with Spock from Star Trek. I write *NOT STAR TREK* next to the name.

"And then later in the sixties, there was the whole nuclear threat. There was a lot of racial tension and mistrust during that time, so everyone was even more on edge. So much violence during the sixties. I was in Texas at the time."

I've heard people talk about the fifties and sixties being a better time in the United States. More family values and a stronger Christian ethic in the country. A time when America was better than it is now. My dad's description makes it sound no different than today.

"Around that time, I was 16, and my mother told me that Mac was raping her."

I wince. I know that my dad's stepfather was violent towards him, but I didn't realize the violence spilled over to my grandmother.

"At one point, I grabbed Mac's shotgun and came at him while he was sleeping. I kicked his bed to wake him up, and I screamed at him. I told him I was going to kill him for what he did to my mom."

I stare at my dad's frail body and delicate hands. His soft green eyes. I can't imagine him yelling at anyone, much less pointing a shotgun and threatening to kill them. My dad was always soft-spoken and gentle. He's kind. But maybe people aren't born with the sort of kindness my dad carries. Maybe kindness is what people choose when they've witnessed horrible things, and they don't want anyone else to experience those same horrors.

"I didn't shoot him. I wanted to. God, I wanted to." He shuts his eyes. The tiny muscles in his jaw protrude when he clenches his teeth. "Instead, I got sent to juvie, and then I got reassigned to a mental institution in Texas."

Juvenile detention. Mental institution. I draw a child behind bars. Were there rehabilitation programs in the sixties? Does my dad talk to counselors who hear and believe his story? Do they understand the situation with his mother? Do they do anything about it? Does the situation become safer for my dad and his mother? The *no* just echoes and repeats on my paper.

"Another year goes by, and the situation at home doesn't improve much, except that Mac directs most of his violence at me instead of my mother. So that was good."

There's that word again. *Good*. A *good* life. How is any of this good?

My dad told me terrible stories of his stepfather's violence before. One story was when my dad complained about the way his mom made a sandwich, causing Mac to fly into a rage and beat him nearly unconscious. Another time, Mac dragged my dad outside to a field and told him to run. Mac raised his shotgun to head level and yelled, "Duck!" My dad had to fall to the ground. Mac would fire the shotgun where my dad was just standing, and my dad would hear the shots zip by above his head. This happened more than once. It was weekend fun for Mac.

"When I was seventeen, my mom said that because I kept starting fights with Mac, I wasn't allowed to stay at the house anymore. She told me to pack my stuff and leave. Just like that. And then she gave me the money to buy a bus ticket to anywhere I wanted to go."

"She made *you* leave? Why? Where did you go?"

"She loved him, I suppose." He shakes his head and takes another puff on his cigarette. "I told her I was going to go to California. That's where all the hippies went. But I wanted to stop in Oklahoma first to see my dad."

The smoke leaves his lips and drifts into the room to join the cloud of death. I never went looking for my dad. When I left my mom and Korea at age sixteen, it wasn't because I was fleeing a violent situation or that she was kicking me out. I demanded to leave so I could come back home to Washington to graduate high school with my friends. I was willing to leave stability to sleep on a couch at friends' houses. And when I returned to my home state, I didn't seek out my dad. I never did.

"Did you talk to your dad much after your parents divorced?"

"No, not really. Some letters, but that's about it. We didn't have Facebook or e-mails back then, so it wasn't easy to know what was going on. On the way to my dad's place, I fell in with some bikers and got robbed blind."

"What?! I didn't know about that. Bikers? What kind of bikers?"

My dad rests his face in his hand and looks up, searching for this memory. "I don't know. Just some bikers." He shrugs.

"Well, at seventeen, you weren't old enough to be in a bar, right? I've always pictured bikers hanging out at bars, with their motorcycles parked next to each other in the gravel out front. You probably didn't get a chance to kick one bike over and knock the rest down like dominoes, huh? Like the movies?"

"No, nothing fun like that," he laughs. "It wasn't at a bar." He doesn't go into further detail and I don't press him for it. It's enough for me that he's able to laugh about a story that involves him getting robbed and possibly beaten up.

"So I finally got to my dad's house. That didn't go over too well."

"Oh. What happened?" I picture my dad fresh out of the fight with the bikers. Maybe he's got a black eye, disheveled hair, and torn jeans. He has a bloody cut on his lip. If that's the scene, maybe his dad thought he was getting into trouble and didn't want to bring that into his house.

My dad doesn't respond for a moment. His eyebrows furl and unfurl, and there is pain in his eyes.

"You don't have to tell me—"

He raises his hand to stop me and then continues speaking. "He told me... I couldn't come in." He inhales and then swallows. His face tenses up, and he exhales. "He said that I couldn't stay there. He didn't even let me in the house." His voice quivers.

"Why?" I'm afraid to ask. I don't want to bring my dad more torment.

"I think it was because Liz was afraid."

Grandma Liz. My dad's stepmother. "Afraid of what?"

"I think she was afraid that if my dad took me in and loved me and housed me, he wouldn't have any love left for her son Joe. She was afraid for her son, so she forced my dad to push me out. Joe got to be my father's son."

The hairs on my arm stand on end. I'm struck by a memory from when I was ten. We lived in the apartments in Steilacoom, and my parents made a big deal about a letter they received from Angie. She was about 17 or 18 then and she wanted to get to know her father. My father. Angie and her full-brother Nathan were dragged through life by a series of violent and abusive men that their mother brought into their home. Unspeakable violence.

It's the same dark cloud that followed my dad. Angie sought out her own father. Like my dad, she was looking for someone to take her in and love her. To shield her from sorrow, but there was an obstacle. A shut door. A defensive wife with her own son. That wife wanted nothing to do with any past children from another marriage. In order to calm his new wife's fears, my dad had to become like his own father. He had to leave behind his past children to move forward with his new family. With me.

I am one of the cogs in the machine of brokenness, rejection, and heartache.

Does my dad view his father as the antagonist in his life story? Or does Mac get all the blame? Does my dad see himself as the source of heartache for his two prior children, or does the blame solely fall on the series of abusive men who filled the void left by our dad?

I wonder if my dad is carrying both the wounds of rejection from his father and the guilt of rejecting and abandoning his own children.

"So, where did you go?"

"I planned to go to California anyway. I blew the bus fair getting to my dad's place, so I hitchhiked to California, and then I started hitching rides everywhere. I went back and forth between San Francisco and Boston. A whole bunch of us hippies fighting against vulture capitalism. We hitched, snuck onto freight trains. It was fun, actually. Mostly fun."

Mostly fun. I know the terrible part of the story. I know that my dad hitched a ride with the wrong person. He got into a semi-truck, and the driver decided that he would have his way with my dad. This violation was another crushing blow to my dad's sense of control over the world. In my dad's life, everything seemed to fall apart, and my dad was alone to pick up the pieces.

My dad doesn't repeat any of that story right now. There are no details here that my dad wants to recall and relive. It is enough for me to know the timeline of my dad's life and where specific mile markers were placed. I write as quickly as I can.

"You know, the hippie movement died because it was too hard," my dad says while laughing, drawing the attention away from the shadow of brokenness. "They all wanted to be self-sustaining. Self-sufficient. They wanted to step outside of that vulture capitalist world so they could figure out how to be free. But guess what? They starved! They ran out of money. They wanted to live outside the system, but there's only so much food in a garbage can!" He laughs again, but my dad isn't laughing *at* them. He's laughing at his own hippie journey. He was one of them. My first bicycle was built as a result of dumpster diving. My dad had experience with this.

For a moment, I thought the hippie life was where my dad found some joy. I thought "peace and love" was the right place for him to recover from his wounds. I'm a bit disheartened by the reality. Scavenging for food doesn't sound like Utopia. Grasping at resources to survive sounds like the same pain and anguish. It sounds like people fending for themselves and trampling on the weak to claw their way to the top. It sounds like the same hell my dad already had to endure.

"At some point, everybody had to rejoin society. The rich kids took up positions in their parents' companies. The same corporations they railed against! Everybody had to find a job. The hippie dream just kind of died."

"What did you do?"

"Well, after nine years of being a hippie, I joined the army."

"Ugh," I protest. "Gross."

"No, no, it was good. Structure, leadership, and learning how people deal with difficulties. It was good for me."

I don't understand how my dad can talk favorably about the Army. I saw copies of letters my dad wrote that mentioned his inability to get promotions because his superiors hated and harassed him. He said they filed complaints about his incompetence and his failure to achieve or thrive. I resented the military ever since.

"Didn't the army kick you out? Dishonorable discharge or something like that?"

"Well," he chuckles. "That was your mom's fault."

I write *Mom?* next to *Army* and wonder if I'll get around to asking her what happened.

Every word I write makes me feel closer to my dad and closer to his pain. Is this normal? Is this what it's supposed to feel like to have a dad around? We're sitting in front of the TV with drinks in hand. I've got my feet propped up on the coffee table, and he's got a cigarette flopping in his lips while he talks. He's sharing stories about his past, and I'm listening like a little kid, enamored by my father's stories.

Another hour has passed. It's eleven o'clock now. There is a break in the conversation, so we're watching the dumbest science-fiction monster movie I've ever seen. On the screen right now is a giant squid grabbing people off a boat's deck and dragging them underwater. There's an absurdity to the scene that's making me laugh inside. It feels perfect.

My dad didn't plan for us to watch this movie together. He didn't know we'd distract ourselves from the darkness with comedic deaths, but it works for me. The next time I'm facing the death of a loved one, I'll have to bring this movie back up and let it draw me away from the heartache.

My dad taps on the couch to get my attention. "They're going to be here in about half an hour, Joshua."

"They?"

"The hospice people. And the Death with Dignity people."

My heart stops. I have to force myself to breathe and be calm.

My dad looks calm. I want to ask my dad if he's nervous, but the question seems wrong.

I study my dad's face while he watches the giant squid drag another screaming victim under the waves. He briefly looks up from the TV and meets my gaze. I think he *is* nervous. But he has said goodbye so many times in life. This probably feels familiar to him.

"Dad, I have a question."

"Ok, shoot."

"I need to know something, and I know I'm not going to have another opportunity to ask this."

"Anything, Joshua."

I've had this question in my mind for thirteen years. This question has been nagging at me, forcing me to tread so carefully in the world as a father raising three children. I wonder about my impact on my kids, and I hope I've done everything I can to raise them with good moral values and a strong but humble sense of identity. I've tried to be a good parent.

I write *Free to Be* on my paper and underline it twice. Three times. Once for each of my daughters. I look up at my dad, and his eyes sparkle. I'm so afraid to ask him.

"Alright, Dad." I take a deep breath. "I raised my three girls to view the world a certain way. I didn't want them to be limited by other people's expectations. I want them to be able to do anything they want. To be whatever they want to be."

"I didn't want my daughters to believe they had to grow up and get *girl* jobs, or that they could only do *girl* things. I raised them to understand that there is no such thing as *boy* jobs or *girl* jobs. I wanted a different world for them." I sink into my dad's eyes. "Different from the one you grew up in."

My dad's expression softens, and he nods slowly. My jaw clenches and unclenches. I click the back of the pen a few times.

"Dad, if you grew up believing that you could be anything and that it was perfectly ok for a little boy to enjoy playing with dolls and collect flowers... and for a young man to be disinterested in football and trucks... if you grew up being told that you could just be you and that you'd be loved regardless, do you think you would have still gone through with it all? Do you think you'd still believe you had to be a woman?"

I drop my head and squeeze my eyes shut. I hear my dad draw in a slow, deep, raspy breath.

I hate myself for asking. I hate having to question him. I hate being unable to cross the threshold of acceptance. The broken question mark I've drawn on the page is filled with pain. Is there a way for me to advocate for my dad when I don't understand? Should I have to understand to accept? As much as my wounds sting from abandonment and self-blame, I *know* that my dad's wounds are greater. If my dad says yes, that his gender identity is wholly separate from the endless years of torment in his life, then I'm the terrible son who isn't able to give my dad what he needs on his dying day. I'm not different than everyone else in my dad's life.

I can't look up from my paper.

"Probably not, Joshua. Probably not."

I shudder and drop my head. The tears that stream down my face are hot. My dad's reply breaks the chains, and I feel the weight that I've carried for twenty years drop from my shoulders.

This world, our terrible world, created a rigid set of rules defining what it means to be *a man*, and then it crushed anyone who didn't obey. When my dad deviated from those rules, it told him he wasn't enough. He didn't live up. He wasn't man enough. My dad couldn't complete *the circle*. The system dragged my dad down to the ground, and it tried to beat him into compliance. And then it blamed my dad for running away from the very system that was trying to kill him, accusing him of abandoning his wife and son.

If my dad didn't believe the lie that he wasn't man enough, he wouldn't have left. He wouldn't have become homeless and an alcoholic. Maybe he wouldn't have needed the tiny moments of escape into the smoke that only cigarettes can provide.

My dad is going to die today. The world's requirements around gender are to blame.

My dad and I sit in silence long enough for me to fill a page with words of fury against the world. I write about the structured roles of men and women in society. I sketch a clenched fist in the middle of the page that grasps the hair of a severed head and write *Goliath* under it. If young David killed and beheaded the giant, there's no reason I can't. For the first time, I feel like I can direct all of my anger away from my dad and towards the system that hurt him. Maybe this is what forgiveness feels like.

The childhood hurts are gone. I smile at my dad and see...

my dad. I see a father who loves me as best he can, despite the injuries he suffered his entire life. And I finally accept that love.

There's a knock on the door, and my blood turns to ice. The clock has struck noon, and the people who threaten to undo the healing are on the other side of that door. Before I can stand up and answer, they knock again, and the room fills with glowing red threads that crisscross the room.

Can I stop them from coming in? Can I convince my dad to change his mind about ending his life? Our relationship just started, and I need more stories. I need to know more about how we're connected. I need to know if these red threads crisscrossing the room are tied to me. I just need more time.

"Come in!" my dad calls out with the same cheerful voice that has greeted every visitor. My heart sinks.

The door swings open, and three figures slip into the room. Phantoms. Their faces are skulls with red glowing eyes that scour the room, looking for someone to devour. I hear the crackle of ice as the room freezes in their wake. They are hungry for my father's soul. *Harvesters.*

"Hi, Anna," a woman says, and the illusion fades.

The woman doesn't look threatening, and there's nothing sinister in her voice. She doesn't have the appearance of a phantom, or a predator, or anyone who wants to do harm. But she called my dad by his other name, and I'm not ready.

She directs her attention to me. "You must be Joshua?"

"Yeah. Josh. I'm his son." I push back against the woman's words. Against the pronoun. If I give in now, the world wins. This is *my* father. This woman is only here to take him away from me. Why should she have any say at all?

"I see. Well. *Anna* has a few things *she* needs to do before we can get started, and I want to make sure we've covered everything. We want to make this go as smoothly and calmly as possible for *her*." She emphasizes while staring me in the eyes. "And for *her* sake, wouldn't it be better if we used *her* correct pronouns?" Her skeletal face reappears, and I shrink back.

I look back at my dad and then at her, and I don't know what's right anymore. The phantoms move closer. Their chants grow louder. The red threads in the room wrap around my wrists and feet and hold me in place, and I'm powerless to struggle or fight back. My hands ball into fists, and I want to yell.

I'm not ready. I just can't. I'm the one losing someone. I'm the one who missed out on having a father my whole life. I'm the one who desperately needs the relationship. She has no right to take this away from me. She doesn't get to define my dad and my relationship with him.

"No," my dad commands, and the earth shakes. He looks at me and then back at her. A rushing wind blows through the room, past me, and across the phantoms. Their black, tattered cloaks are blown back by the power of my dad's word. "Joshua should call me *Dad*. I'm his father. I'm not his mother. It's appropriate for my son to refer to me as *him*."

The threads burn away like twine, and I slump to the ground. I raise my head to meet my dad's gaze and tremble at the weary grace in his eyes. I'm so weak. I look away before I weep.

The woman purses her lips in protest at first but then nods in reluctant agreement. She motions to one of the two men with her, and he joins her. The other man holds a medical bag and remains motionless near the door.

The first two approach my dad and sit next to him. I turn away to stare out the sliding glass window and listen to them alternate between questions.

The woman starts. "Do you wish to proceed with physician-assisted suicide of your own volition?"

I silently beg my dad to say no.

"Yes," my dad replies.

The man asks my dad the next question. "Do you want to have more time to consider your decision?"

Please, Dad. Please.

"No," he says.

The woman asks the next one. "Is there any aspect of your care or alternatives you would like to discuss further?

God, please. Do something. Please, I'm begging you.

"No," he says again.

The woman says thank you to my dad, and the two of them stand up from the couch and look around the apartment like they're trying to find something. The woman peers down the hall, shakes her head and turns back, and then the man points to a spot on the kitchen floor. They nod and whisper back and forth. The man standing in the kitchen by the door says nothing.

"We want to make a comfortable spot on the floor for you to lie down," the woman says to my dad. "You have blankets and cushions here with you that should work. Do you have a pillow?"

My dad points to the hallway, and I rush to the bedroom and edge past the large cardboard boxes and piles of clothes on the floor. I grab one of the pillows from the bed and bring it back to the living room. The woman and man are laying blankets on the floor, and I hand the pillow to the woman. I step back and look at the final place my dad will rest before he passes. A pile of blankets on the kitchen floor.

"It's much easier if he's already lying down," the woman tries to reassure me. "That way, we don't have to move him so much. After."

"Yeah, ok."

They spend the next few minutes helping my dad from the couch to the floor. It's painful to watch, and when I try to help, they tell me this is their responsibility. I can't do anything but stand and see my dad wince in pain as they hold him by his arms and walk him to the kitchen floor. He breathes a sigh of relief when they finally get him to the floor.

The two of them stand back and nod to the third man, who still hasn't spoken.

"Ok, the two of us are going to step outside now," the woman says. "We can't stay in the room while the medication is prepared."

Before I can ask what she means, my dad explains. "Death with Dignity. It's legal in Oregon, but it's also *not entirely* legal. There are some... rules to make it work."

Rules for dying. I nod at the absurdity of the words.

"We can come back once he's done," she says, and the two hospice care staff leave. Once the door shuts, I feel a chill air rush through the apartment. One phantom remains in the room with us. He is the Death with Dignity doctor. The doctor of death.

I wrestle with this term, "death with dignity." It's the name of the organization that carries out these physician-assisted suicides, as they're called, but where is the dignity here, exactly? I stare at the bed on the floor. And do people who die without the help of doctors have any less dignity? Are their deaths less worthy of respect?

The doctor's voice breaks the strange silence. "Where do you keep your cups, Anna?" He stands near the cupboards, and his hand hovers over each handle like he's unwilling to open one without permission.

My dad points to the correct cupboard door. The doctor opens it and retrieves one of the four identical navy blue coffee mugs, and then sets it on the counter. His movements are slow. Purposeful.

He reaches into his duffel bag and pulls out a small jug of orange juice and a pill bottle. He grabs the mug and the pill bottle and sits on the floor beside my dad. Without looking up, he opens the bottle. One by one, he splits each capsule and catches the pink powder in the navy blue coffee mug.

"You have to open every capsule?"

"Yes."

"How many are in there?"

"There's one hundred."

One hundred capsules filled with pink powdery death. I study the phantom in front of me. He wears glasses and has graying blonde hair. He's thin, and his clothes hang awkwardly from his frame as he's hunched over splitting capsules. He is sitting with his legs crossed on the floor in clean brown slacks. They're going to get a little dirty.

How does a doctor get into the business of death? How do they decide that their purpose is to end life instead of preserve it? *Primum non nocere.* First, do no harm. Isn't that the oath of doctors? The doctor's world is suspended in this strange place between living and dying. Between ending suffering for my dad and causing it for me.

I stare at the doctor while he works. He twists each capsule apart and empties the contents. Capsule after capsule after capsule.

Halfway through the pill bottle, my dad speaks. "Is there a way I can get... something? Something to take the edge off?" I can see his hand trembling.

The doctor nods, saying nothing, and he reaches into his bag again. He retrieves a syringe and asks my dad if he can do it himself. My dad says he can, so the doctor hands him the syringe.

I look away. It seems private, so I wait until I can tell my dad is done.

It's not like I imagined. I thought it would be like a drug addict injecting heroin and then slipping into a half-conscious dreamlike state. But I don't notice anything different about my dad. He exhales heavily and then sets the syringe down next to him.

When all the capsules are split and poured into the mug, the doctor fills it with orange juice and stirs. It's a concoction of death. A fatal beverage in a coffee mug.

"You're going to want to drink this all quickly. It tastes terrible. It's thick, but we don't want to dilute it any more than this."

I study the doctor's face and I wonder how many times he has done this. How many capsules has he broken open, mixed with juice, and handed out? How many people have died under his care?

1:51 p.m.

My dad struggles to drink the potion. He gags and screws up his face. He looks genuinely upset for the first time, and I want to take the mug from him and drink it myself. It takes several attempts for him to finish it, and when he does, I can't stop my tears.

There is a lethal dose of poison inside my dad. That poison is violence, and we are the ones who filled that cup. The poison is contempt. It is hatred and intolerance and rejection, mixed together in a pink slurry.

When he's done, the doctor knocks on the apartment door, and the hospice care staff come back into the room.

Your father is going to die.

My dad reaches for my hand and gently squeezes it. I blink through the tears.

"The first place I want to visit when I die is Turtle Heaven."

"Turtle… Heaven?" I wipe tears from my face. I've never heard my dad mention Turtle Heaven before.

"Yeah. Turtle Heaven. God told me that my turtles would be ok in Turtle Heaven. I want to see them."

"Did you have a lot of turtles die?" I don't know this story. The only turtle death I knew was turtle Randy, and I'm still letting myself believe he might be around.

"Oh, yeah. Lots. I had so many turtles, Joshua. I loved every single one of them."

I can't tell if he's already delirious from the medication. His eyes are closed, but he opens them and continues.

"When I was really little, I collected box turtles from the field out back and brought them into the house. I'd put them in rows in front of the TV, and I'd pretend like they were in a drive-in theater. We'd watch movies together in the house." He laughs. "I really identified with them. They could hide away in their little shells, like houses. No matter where they were, they were home. I wanted to feel like that."

I can see the turtles in front of the TV and a little boy behind them. He's lying on the floor with his head in his hands, barely watching the movie. He's focused on each of the turtles. He keeps scooting them back in place to keep them from wandering off and getting lost in the house.

"But those weren't the turtles that died, Joshua. After movie time, I would always let them back outside so they could go live the rest of their lives. It was the snapping turtles that died."

"Snapping turtles?" My dad never talked about snapping turtles except to warn me about the strength of their bites. He said they could easily take your finger clean off with a single bite. He once told me that a full-grown snapping turtle could bite through a wooden broom handle.

"Mac would take me fishing. He loved fishing, but every now and then, a small snapping turtle would grab the hook, and it would make Mac so mad. He would take his knife and slit the turtle's neck and toss the dead turtle back into the water."

"Oh my gosh, dad."

"And he would make me watch. Every single time. He knew I loved turtles. He knew."

My dad stays quiet for a bit. I have no words of comfort. There is nothing that can make sense of this madness.

"I didn't know what to do with all that pain and hurt, so I just kept it inside. I grew up coping with drugs and alcohol. Golf, too. And then, after a while, I didn't think about the turtles again. I suppose I just carried the souls of those turtles around so deep inside of me that I didn't have to worry about it."

My dad's turtles. All the little shelled creatures that were cruelly killed by a heartless stepdad became his trauma and brokenness. Innocence slain. They were helpless. They became his helplessness.

"But then, do you know what happened? One winter, when you were just a little boy... we were at the apartment in Steilacoom. There was a big snowstorm, and we had eighteen inches of snow. The neighbors built a giant igloo, and you—"

"—I built that snow turtle."

"Yeah! That snow turtle..." He pauses and looks around the room and squints. He stares at his hands. At me. The medication is starting to devour him. "Joshua, when I saw that snow turtle, it was like God gave me a message. He told me that your little snow turtle was a memorial for all of those turtles that died. He was going to take care of them and bring them all into Turtle Heaven. God said He wasn't going to let them die for nothing. He was going to take them into Turtle Heaven. That's where I needed them to go. In that snow turtle, God answered my childhood prayers, Joshua. I'm going to Turtle Heaven first."

My dad squeezes my hand and closes his eyes. With his head turned, the tears run down the side of his face and onto his pillow. He breathes heavily and doesn't speak again. The Death with Dignity folks tell me that my dad is such a fighter, and that death usually occurs after 15 minutes. It's been twenty-five minutes already. He seems so peaceful.

2:35 p.m.

Good night, dad.

I'm holding the limp hand of my father in mine with our fingers gently intertwined when his heart finally stops beating.

I want there to be a sweetness to the passing. I want to see a butterfly flying up from somewhere in the room and out the window like a gentle spirit lifted into heaven. But that doesn't happen now. I just feel all the muscles in my body tensing, bracing for the heartache that I know is going to come. I try to prepare myself for what comes next.

Sometimes, grief is slow. It's a fog that rolls in while you're keeping busy with things to distract yourself. You're at work, or eating a meal, or reading a book, and then you look up and you can't see past the heavy thickness of the air. It engulfs you. The pain swallows you and everything you love in its cold and wet embrace. It blots out the sun, and you struggle to find any hope.

But grief is not slow today. Today, grief is a raging juggernaut. The apartment door crashes open and explodes into splinters. The whole room has burst open in violence. The beast of grief smashes every wall, pounds the ceiling until the roof is thrown off the building, and the air is sucked out of the room. The sliding glass door is millions of broken pieces of glass that rip into my soul. This beast, grown from decades of pain and betrayal and abandonment and hopelessness, rampages and threatens to destroy everything in the world. The tears pour down my face. I want the beast to crush me, too.

As the world splinters and howls, I text Kendra. Each letter I type is anguish. *He's gone. You should come.* My family arrives within minutes.

The room is a hurricane of tears. My mom, Kendra, the girls. Uncontrollable weeping. The medical staff check my dad's pulse a couple more times to make sure that he's really dead, but my own heartbeat is pounding so loudly I have to look away. I walk to the sliding glass door and step outside into the rain.

I try to drift into daydream. I yearn to conjure forest or fairy dust or anything to take me away, but every drop of rain that lands on me grounds me in reality. I'm the only one who showed up for my dad. Not Steve, the caregiver, who wouldn't heed my dad's request to take the gecko. Not my sister, who said she would take time off work to be here. And not Curtis, my dad's one friend who promised to be here today. I'm the only one.

Would it be better if more people attended my dad's death? Did I want to spend the last minutes of my dad's life listening to other people talk about their own lives? Perhaps I would have missed the final details of my dad's story. I would have missed getting to know him.

I come back inside and my family still surrounds my dad. He looks so peaceful on the floor. No more struggling to breathe. No more painful fits of coughing. He looks like he's sleeping.

I keep looking, just in case he wakes up. Maybe he's just hibernating, and he'll wake up next spring.

Acceptance

"Today was his last day."

"So he's gone? Just like that?"

"I said that. You already know. You were there."

"I know. I'm just making conversation."

"It's fine. It is what it is."

"So... what do you do now?"

"I dunno. I keep telling myself that I haven't had a dad since I was a little kid. I'm grieving, but it makes me feel bad for anybody who's lost a parent that they had a good relationship with. Am I allowed to grieve? It's weird."

"Yeah, I get what you're saying. Your feelings are real, though. You did lose someone. Maybe we can talk through what that means."

"What it means? I don't know. But it feels like I lost... an idea. Or a possibility. There's a locked door, and I lost the key. I lost the possibility of a relationship that I could have had. I didn't lose a father-son relationship. I lost the ability to ever have one."

"But you did have a father-son relationship. You just had your own. Every father-son relationship is different, right?"

"Sure, but I'm sure most of them involve more activities together. Doing stuff. I don't know. I don't know what sons are supposed to do with their fathers!"

"I don't know, either. But you had a dad who actually loved you. He wanted you by his side at the end. Most people who say they don't have a father-son relationship have an absent father who never returns. Or they've never even met their father."

"I know. This is different, though. Once I really got to be with him, he's gone. I get to live the rest of my life as a person without a father. This just feels so weird. I hate this."

"I hate it, too. We can hate it together. Oh, by the way, I wanted to say I'm sorry."

"For what?"

"For earlier, when I gave you grief about your dad's pronouns. I didn't know that he wanted you to use male pronouns for him. I mean, I just thought you were being insensitive or cruel to your dad, but I guess there was something else there. Something special."

"Yeah. I didn't know, either. I mean, I'm so glad about it. You have no idea how much of a weight that lifted off my shoulders. Maybe I was being insensitive, though. Or weak? Like, I couldn't bring myself to ever call my dad *she*. I dunno."

"Going forward, that's probably going to make some people uncomfortable. Talking about your trans dad with his old pronoun is a bit like dead-naming, isn't it? People get pretty upset about that."

"Whatever. They can be upset. He wasn't their dad. It's not their story."

"Well, just remember to be kind. Imagine if your dad didn't want you to call him by male pronouns. What if it was really important to him, and he asked you to switch it? If you held your ground, I don't know if I'd take your side on that. Identity is important to people. You can't just ignore that."

"In that case, I'm glad that my dad felt the way he did. That's what he said, and that's the version of the story I want to stick with."

"Ok."

"You good with that?"

"I don't see how I can argue about it."

"Great. So, anyhow, what do I do now? Do you think something is supposed to be different? Am I supposed to have changed in some profound way?"

"Do you feel different?"

"Right now? I don't think so. But I think I'll feel different in the future. After I've had some time to really process it."

"Well, when you're ready, you'll have to write a book about it."

Out to Sea

Summer, 2017.

The overcrowded excursion ship finally slowed at the place the captain called *Turtle Bay*. Tourists from all over the world scurried about the deck, eager to see beneath the waves. At the rear of the ship, people donned their diving suits and snorkels. One by one, they jumped off the deck of the ship into the clear ocean water off the coast of Maui.

The locals in Maui said that every bay was the famous Turtle Bay. It's just a thing these boat captains and excursion coordinators said to sound exclusive, like they were the only ones who knew the secret hiding places of the magnificent sea creatures. Anything for a buck. In truth, there were dozens of places to see the turtles.

Josh dangled his feet in the water and shook his head back at his wife.

"It's pretty cold, Kendra. I don't think you're gonna like

this."

"I already told you I wasn't going in. Libby's too scared, so I'll stay here with her. You can take the other two," Kendra said while helping Charlie into a tiny suit. Olivia was already suited up and ready to jump in.

"Can I get in the water, Dad?" Olivia begged, jumping in place.

"Hang on, hang on. Wait until Charlie is ready so we can go in together. Libby, are you absolutely sure?"

Libby stared at her feet and nodded, and Josh wondered if she would regret missing another fun excursion on this vacation. He looked at Kendra, who nodded back at him and shooed him off the deck with her hands.

"Hurry up and go in, Josh. It'll be fine. Go see the turtles."

Josh and two of his daughters jumped into the water and were immediately transfixed by the brilliant seascape.

The water was so clear they could see the nearly florescent sea anemone on the floor and all the brightly colored fish between them. Tiny pipefish dangled like white Christmas lights near the surface and sparkled just the same. And there were turtles. A few of them. Some tourists surrounded them and were taking pictures with their bulky waterproof cameras.

The turtles were much smaller than Josh expected. He was familiar with leatherback turtles, which could grow up to seven feet long. He imagined swimming next to one and taking hold of its shell to let it pull him through the water. These little green sea turtles were only a couple of feet long. Tiny in comparison, but still so beautiful.

Josh popped up near the surface to take another breath and then dove back down again. He saw Olivia pointing at a pair of large black and white fish swimming next to each other, and he gave her a thumbs up. Curious how deep he could swim, Josh took a deep breath from the surface and dove straight down to the sea floor. Up close, the sea anemones were even more vibrant. Crabs scurried on the rocky ground. He stretched out his hand to touch the ground before swimming back up to the surface. Once at the top, he took another deep breath and dove again. This time, he wanted to see if he could swim under the width of the excursion ship. Swimming under a large boat sounded fascinating.

When he finally returned to the ship's rear, he heard Kendra yelling for him. He turned and saw Kendra frantically pointing at the water in the distance.

He pulled the snorkel away from his face and hollered to her. "What's the matter?"

"Charlie is out there!" Kendra yelled. Her eyes were a mix of fear and anger.

"What? Where?" Josh turned and tried to see, but the waves were too high to see anything. "And where's Olivia?"

Kendra yelled back to Josh. "Olivia is back on the boat already. She said she was too cold. Charlie's drifting out to sea!"

Josh still couldn't see his youngest daughter through the waves, so he ducked under the surface and swam quickly in the direction his wife pointed, fighting against the panic with every swim stroke.

And then he saw her. Charlie was calmly face-down at the surface with her snorkel poking out of the water. She was in the perfect position to swim without having to lift her head at all. She was letting herself drift, slowly kicking her feet and moving further away from the boat and her family to follow a lone turtle that no one else noticed.

Charlie was safe, but if Josh didn't stop her, she might have followed the turtle into the wide open ocean.

A father adoring his son and a son adoring his father

Note: BioGift Anatomical

I reached out to BioGift Anatomical to find out exactly what happened to my dad's body. They were kind enough to send me a letter in 2024 that gave some details. The letter refers to my dad as my "Mother," which was a little jarring when I first saw it, but I understand why they wrote it that way. In any event, it's neat to know that my dad was able to help with LifeFlight and Weill Cornell Medical College.

BioGift
Anatomical
Your final gift could last for generations

Dear Samantha Culley family,

We offer you our heartfelt condolences for the loss of your Mother. We hope that the generous gift of Samantha's body for the benefit of future generations brings you all comfort. There is no greater gift, and it will be viewed as an important and lasting memorial to helping others.

BioGift acquires as much medical information as we can from the donor's family, personal physician, or other facilities. Coupled with the donor's age, weight and other medical criteria, an assessment is made based on this information, plus the current medical science need, to maximize the gift. While no guarantee can be given due to unforeseen circumstances, consideration is always applied to a directed donation whereby the family wishes to prioritize how the gift is used. All researchers and educators must complete a stringent application and the use must be approved prior to receiving any specimens from BioGift. This ensues that all uses honor the donor, have merit, and fall within the general public's mainstream idea of good medical research and educational use.

Tissues recovered from Samantha were reserved, or already placed for a good portion of the following medical purposes:
- An educational facility which trains LifeFlight Network on in-field training to prepare them for any situation they may face.
- An educational facility involved in the research of the brain at Weill Cornell Medical College.

The above medical science endeavors are cutting edge and remarkable. However, without a gift such as Samantha gave, they are highly improbable or even impossible at this time to complete. It is a special gift and facilitates the progress of medical science for future generations. Thank you.

Sincerely,
BioGift Anatomical, Inc.

Note: On the Subject of Gender

Gender is a delicate subject. This story wasn't written to cast an opinion, but rather to simply share a story of something that happened. It's the story that addresses one person's gender journey and the impact it had on the family around them.

There are people who experience gender dysphoria differently than the way I described in this novel, and while I can't speak to their experiences, I believe their stories are just as real and valid.

Note: Inheritance

In the novel, I mentioned that I inherited around $3,000 from my dad. This is true, but it's not all I inherited. I adopted Deuce, the leopard gecko. Serendipitously, my dad was wrong about the gecko's gender! It turns out Deuce is a female leopard gecko, and as of May 21, 2024, she's doing quite well. Apparently, they can live for 15 to 20 years, and I've had her for eight. She usually hangs out in a little cave I designed and 3D-printed for her. My dad also had a small rock collection, and those rocks make up a part of the gecko's habitat.

I also inherited my dad's "bug-out bag." I like to imagine that if my dad survived long enough to see Trump win the election, he would have taken his bag and ventured into the woods to live out the rest of his days off-grid. The bag had a collection of knives, rope, flashlights, gardening tools, lots of smaller bags, and some weird things like ninja throwing stars and decorative short sword. Because why not?

There was a KA-BAR in the mix, which made it my dad's only good knife. New, it's just under a hundred bucks, which would have been a lot of money for my dad. I don't know the story behind it, but I assume it was part of a trade or something. My dad loved flea markets and bartering. This particular KA-BAR is a "fighting/utility" knife, and even though it's the short version with a 5.25" blade, it's really sturdy. The black-painted carbon steel blade holds an edge remarkably well, and it's quite intimidating. My dad probably should have thrown away all of his other knives and just kept this one.

I have the Alien Abduction Survival Handbook on my bookshelf next to me. It's an absurd book, but it's fun to flip through. My dad also had a Wilderness Survival book which contains *actual* useful information for outdoor survival, so maybe he would have been ok in the woods.

Acknowledgments

This was my first novel. I started writing Turtle Heaven in 2018 during the annual National Novel Writing Month challenge, two years after my dad passed away. I didn't figure out a direction for the writing, so I shelved the story for the next several years. I picked it up again at the end of 2023 when I decided to commit to a single project. From December 2023 to May 2024, I focused my creative efforts into completing the one project that mattered to me: telling the story of reconciliation between me and my dad.

I shed tears writing this book. I didn't know healing could occur while sharing my pain, but somehow, writing and rewriting the scenes gave me a sense of control over how the stories affected me. I learned I could decide what lessons I wanted to learn from my past. Maybe this book will help someone else do the same.

I need to thank my wife. She's a rock. She's was my steady ground and reliable friend while I wrote this book, even when she side-eyed me from the couch when I spent too much time writing instead of spending time with her. She is the most understanding and patient person I've ever met, and I can't thank her enough.

About the Author

Joshua Culley and his family live in Washington State after their seven-year stint in California. Once they moved back to Washington, they spent about nine months living in that RV, and later lived on a boat for fourteen months in the Puget Sound.

The insurance industry keeps writing his paychecks, but Josh's real passion is found in his hobbies. He's still trying to figure out what he wants to do with his life.

Josh is working on his next novel: The House with the Broken Walls. This story will be about the heartache of parenting.

To learn more about Josh and discover more **NEWPROTEST Publishing** authors and books, visit our website: www.newprotest.org

Made in the USA
Middletown, DE
21 August 2024